TEN STEPS

FROM THE
HOTEL INGLATERRA

Annette

Enjoy the book!
It's my baby

Linda Gunther

BY

LINDA S. GUNTHER

A Woman's Romantic Adventure
In Havana, Cuba

- A LIFE-INSPIRED WORK OF FICTION-

Ten Steps From The Hotel Inglaterra is a work of fiction. Names, characters places, and incidents either are the product of the author's imagination or are used fictitiously. Any resemblance to actual persons, living or dead, events or locales is entirely coincidental.

Cover design by Julie Tipton.

ISBN: 0615845320
ISBN 13: 9780615845326

This book is dedicated to my dear brother -
Ron Springhorn, who like me, will always
remember and appreciate the free spirits
of both our mother and sister.

Special thanks to the many contributors -
including: Colin Bunnell, Colleen Garnett,
Pam DeBarr, Kelly DeBarr, Andy Couterier,
Julie Tipton, and Valerie Beeck, who all blessed
me with their invaluable feedback and encouraged
me to complete this romantic-adventure story
and realize my dream to see it published.

You have plenty of courage, I am sure,"

answered Oz.

"All you need is confidence in yourself. There is no

living thing that is not afraid when it faces danger.

The true courage is in facing danger when you are

afraid, and that kind of courage you have in plenty."

L. Frank Baum (Wizard of Oz)

TEN STEPS

FROM THE
HOTEL INGLATERRA

BY
LINDA S. GUNTHER

Chapter One

DOUG — MY PARTNER

"**S**pit it out. Spit it out Clyde." I'm jarred. Trying to park the car. My cell phone screams to be answered. I stop BB King and Eric Clapton in mid-sentence. My dog is choking on something in the passenger seat. I have a major client call in ten minutes and I think that part of my dry cleaning has just blown across the street, out of my convertible. "Shit! Clyde!" I shake him a little. He gives a basset hound gag, coughs and expectorates the slimy object. Where the hell did that come from? What is it? Was it from the cleaners? Changing focus, I panic when I see I'll miss Doug's call. It's the final ring before voicemail. Doug Adams, my partner, my true partner. Only two years into this consulting business and we are rockin'. Stressed out, I'm jittery. I want to talk to him before I get on the phone with Amco, our potential new mega client.

"Doug?" The sound of his voice careens through the car radio speaker. He speaks in a hurried pace. Doug – always upbeat and assertive, the ultimate sales wizard. Enthusiasm overload. He drives us as a dynamic duo, leveraging my insights like a Cadillac salesman in a showroom. He knows exactly what to highlight and when to highlight it. Doug, the consulting champion. I love the energy he has. He's captivating with our clients. "Charlie, are you ready for Amco? Where are you pumpkin? Home?" He sounds far away. I struggle to get Clyde to jump out of the car, get my

keys out, then open my front door; while holding my dry cleaning, my purse, my briefcase, the grocery bag and the cell phone
between my ear and shoulder. Door open, I tumble into the
house. Hurdling over to the kitchen counter, I rip the steaks out
of the grocery bag and throw them onto the plate for thawing;
then crash with my phone still at my ear, onto the couch. I grab
the Amco file from my briefcase and flip it open.

"Doug, one question, how should I position the Employee
Engagement Survey with these guys? I mean, I just want to be clear
on the overall rationale for them doing this thing. It's the pending
acquisition, right? That's the gestalt of it. They should do it for both
sides. Oh shit – Clyde get out of there! God damn – Clyde's got the
steaks. My brother is coming for dinner." I whisk the steaks off
the floor into the sink. Doug chuckles a little. "Breathe, breathe,"
he says with a calm confident air. "Sit down a moment. Gather
yourself. You *know* the rationale. You're the genius on this. Doing
the satisfaction survey with employees globally from both companies will give Amco 'gold' in terms of the cultural temperature;
and help them find out what makes employees tick. Then they'll
have concrete data to help make the right decisions on employee
benefits, compensation policy; what's important to people. Also,
have them think about the streamlining they can do which will
translate into dollars saved. Are you ready Charlie? You have the
power point. You emailed it to Jameson at Amco, right?" Relieved,
I sit on the couch.

"Yes, I'm ready. You're right. I better go Doug. Ten minutes to
the call. I wish you could have made this meeting with me. But I
know you're getting on the plane in a few minutes."

"Love you Charlie. I'll call you later as soon as I can."

It's 5:30 in the afternoon. The Amco meeting is over. I pour
a deserved reward into my glass. The red liquid slides smoothly
down my throat. I seem to enjoy the merlot just a little too much.
Clyde is sleeping on the rug. I float across the room, glass in
hand and turn on the tunes. Oh my God, it's Hotel California; a
golden oldie. I stare out the window at the gray Pacific Ocean. It's

windy now at the beach. The weather has turned from sunshine to overcast and it's now getting dark. I hear the cell phone ring out. It's Doug's signature ring I've arranged on my phone; a few blues notes from BB King.

"Doug?"

"Hi honey, yeah it's me." He sounds tired. "I just landed in Frankfurt. Connecting flight is delayed two hours. Big surprise, right? So? So? Tell me. How did it go with Amco?"

I take another sip of wine. Clyde awakes and picks up his fuzzy green octopus, ready to play. Of course, only when I'm on the phone is he in the mood for play. I throw the toy across the room for him to retrieve.

"Well, I'm kind of down," I timidly respond to Doug. "You know, sometimes I just can't articulate what I'm thinking so clearly in my head."

"Oh," he says, "it didn't go well?" He's let down, but still supportive. "It's okay sweetie. We'll get the next one. We've got scads of clients in the wings who need..."

Interrupting, I burst into a slate of giggles. "*Not!* We got the deal Doug! I nailed it! And, they accepted our $150K bid for a comprehensive global survey." I sing my delight into the phone. "We are the champions! We are the champions!"

Enthusiastically, he responds with, "You are the master, my lovely, bright, sparkling Charlotte Sweeney. And Clyde, he is one lucky animal tonight. Wish I were there to celebrate with you guys. He continues. "Listen - I have a special plan for us, a delicious idea on how we can celebrate in style. We start this Amco gig mid-January, so we have three weeks clear coming up here at Christmas. Let's spend it together in Maui. My kids will be there part of the time, with Monica. But then we'll have several days through New Year's all to ourselves, in a deluxe ocean front, top of the line condo. Just you, me and the gentle sounds of the Napili waves."

I swallow hard because what I'm about to say may not go over well. "Doug, I want to take a trip to Cuba for the holidays." A big sigh over the phone. "Just listen to me - please. Carla's been talking about Cuba. Her Aunt Tessy recently travelled there and says it's an incredible setting for street and people photography. You know I'm a sucker for this stuff. I love the challenge of this kind of adventure. It would energize me. Havana sounds like a great shoot. I'd like to spend two weeks there." Silence on the other side. "Doug, you could come with me if you like, but I'm okay on my own." More silence on the other end. He's rarely without words. Airport announcements in the background. It is a struggle at vacation time between us. I'm craving an adventure trip somewhere I've never been before and Doug is longing to relax in luxury. It's our usual dance. "Doug, listen, you go to Maui. It's already your plan. Your kids will be there. You get that condo and I'll meet you in Maui for New Year's Eve. We can spend a long weekend lounging on the beach."

He finally grunts and says, "I want you to enjoy your holiday time Charlie. It's certainly well deserved. It's just that with me living in Seattle and you in Santa Cruz, we don't see each other enough as it is. December holiday time was our one opportunity."

"I know," I say, understanding how he feels.

He continues, "Sweetie, I wanted to talk to you about us actually living in one locale – together; as a couple. It's time for us, and our consulting partnership makes it even more compelling." I'm taken aback by him dropping the idea of us living together.

"Anyway, I'm sure it's not legal to enter Cuba as a U.S. citizen without a special arrangement - like an educational visa or something like that. You don't have that, right?"

"No," I say.

He continues, "That's what I thought. Isn't it couched as trading with the enemy for goodness sakes? Whatever! It's a hefty fine if you're caught. Sounds risky Charlie. Cuba, sweetie, why?"

I'm feeling pushed to the wall; on the spot here. As I respond, I'm starting to question my own motivation for a trip without Doug at holiday time.

"I don't know Doug. I'm just totally intrigued by this idea. I love Cuban food, Cuban music, and it's a place I've never seen nor photographed. You know I long for adventure travel."

"Yup, I know you love it," he mumbles.

"I'd like to photograph it and then write about it. Cuba is a little dream I've had for awhile; number one on my bucket list. And it's not so forbidden. Knowledgeable Americans do it carefully. Look, once I get this fantasy played out, I'll be 150% ready for the Amco ride and for our other plans for the New Year; including a possible Doug-Charlie household merger."

Doug brightens up and then laughs out loud. "You got it baby! Quite the sales guru – aren't you? Ok, let's plan for New Year's Eve together, with our toes in the fine sands of Maui, and a bottle of even fine champagne. Listen, I'm going to grab a bite before this next flight. I'll buzz you when I hit terra firma in Seattle. I love you Charlie."

Chapter Two

CARLA — MY BEST FRIEND

I ring Carla after I hang up with Doug; leave a quick voicemail to confirm our meeting at the beach in the morning for our weekly dog walk. Carla - my friend for almost eight years. We actually dated the same guy almost at the same time when we worked at Focus Technologies. I was the Human Resources Manager for the division. Carla was the IT Manager. I remember standing in the quarterly company meeting and noticing that she had on the same shoes and almost the same blouse I was wearing. Strange. About a week later, I'm at dog training school with Clyde. I see six foot tall, slender Carla who is usually cool and confident, begging her hefty black lab Sadie to get off the trainer's foot. Clearly embarrassed with Sadie's dog manners, she tugged on the leash as Sadie seemed to press down even harder on the trainer's foot. As Carla desperately tried to untangle Sadie's leash from the trainer's leg, I caught her eye, and we both cracked up laughing.

Our dogs bonded that summer, as did the two of us; as best friends. When we discovered that we had also once dated the same guy – each for exactly two short weeks, we agreed that he never stopped talking about himself; distasteful to each of us. This common link and similar reaction to his narcissistic nature brought us even closer together.

Carla has been an inspiration to me – funny, sarcastic, naughty and nice; all at the same time. You always know where you stand with her. She can immediately command a room with her inner strength; her charismatic presence. And Carla can fix anything – showers, sinks, vacuum cleaners, dish washers. With her forte in IT, she is remarkable in troubleshooting laptop issues or dealing with any computer catastrophe. I call her "the mistress of machines."

Since dating Doug for the past two years and now teamed with him in the consulting business, I can sense Carla's discomfort with him. And truthfully, we haven't had as much time together as "before" Doug. She distrusts him. Although she never speaks of him with explicit negativity, I notice the narrowing of her eyes when I describe Doug's viewpoints. Kind of a wince and wondering smirk on her face when I mention his name. She knows that Doug is still close with his ex-wife Monica, and it bothers Carla; seemingly more than it irks me. I always feel that Carla is looking out for me; always willing to go the extra mile for her closest friends.

This morning I meet Carla at the Rio Del Mar beach entrance to walk with our dogs. Clyde and Sadie take off chasing each other with abandoned exuberance. We make our way to the shoreline. Carla picks up a big stick from the sand and throws it into the ocean. Sadie and Clyde jump with delight, first going for the bouncing stick; then more focused on playing with each other. It seems like a game of tag. I can see them simultaneously spot a sea otter on its back in the waves. Their excitement is obvious. Playfully splashing and jumping about everywhere; they cover every square inch of the area. It's a crisp, clear Northern California day all around. Perfect for a long and chatty walk between intimate friends.

"So, Doug is off to Maui this weekend and you are all set for a photographer's paradise in Havana, Cuba?"

I nod with eager anticipation. "It was you Carla. You inspired me to even consider Cuba as my next adventure destination. So here's my plan. Catch a flight to Cancun, Mexico. Stay a few nights there, pretending that's my final holiday destination. Three days after arrival, I appear at the airport's Cubana Air ticket counter in Cancun, and "on the spot," book a flight to Havana. I don't use my passport but instead have them stamp a white piece of paper, leaving no trace of me officially flying into Cuba." I pause and take a breath. Carla hits me playfully on my shoulder.

"You go girl! Impressive. Sadie. Sadie, get away from that blanket. Sadie, come here girl." She watches over her dog like a treasured child. Sadie obeys and jaunts over to acknowledge her master; then runs back to Clyde, splish-splashing in the water. Carla picks up another large stick and tosses it into the surf, yelling, "Sadie, Clyde, hey – go after this one you two ragamuffins." Carla's throw is impressive.

"Whoa," I say, "are you playing for the Giants next Spring? Quite an arm you got there."

Carla stops and stages a bow in honor of her demonstrated prowess. "So, you've got your plan for Havana and exactly how you described it is how My Aunt Tessy did it too. Same deal. And I hear it's only a 45 minute flight from Cancun to Havana. Just be careful Charlie. Don't use a credit card anywhere. Otherwise you can be tracked. And I hear they're clamping down on offenders."

Carla's long, thick, black ponytail swings back and forth as we walk at a fast pace to catch up to our dogs.

"Right," I say, "cash at the airport, the hotel, in restaurants and shops. I need to make sure I have a pile of cash. Oh, and extra batteries for my Nikon – just in case. I hear it's tough to get that kind of stuff in Havana. What about clothes? What should I take?"

Confident, Carla waves her hand, "Oh that's easy. I'll help you pick out some gems from your closet. You'll be sexy but simple, ready to face humidity with humility. I laugh at her entertaining wit. I admire it. "Who knows, you may run into a sexy Latin Prince Charming." Sí sí?" She swings her hips to some imaginary Cuban music.

Frowning, I place my hands on my hips, giving her the evil eye. I think that's a jab at Doug.

"Think strappy little dresses and tank tops." Carla deflects and continues to talk about clothing options for me.

Suddenly, I'm far away. I slow my pace on the beach. I can feel my shoulders hunch down. It just hits me. Tears well up "out of the blue." I stop walking and blurt out, "maybe Cuba is just an unnecessary fiasco. Doug doesn't like the idea. I should probably just go to Maui with him and we can get ready for January's Amco project together. It will be the start of three months of non-stop business calls, flights and presentations." My stomach is in knots as I say this. Carla grabs my arm and pulls me to the sand, sitting me up against a giant washed up log of wood.

"You **want** Cuba. You're excited; passionate about this trip. Don't pass up an adventure. You'll regret it." Then she changes her tone to a more tender one. "Charlie, it's been a year now, hasn't it?"

I nod. "Yes, one year and three days since my sister's death," I murmur.

Carla comforts me, now hugging my sleeve. "This trip will help you take your mind off Priscilla."

"I know it will." I eek out, "Honestly, I hope it helps to seal this anguish I've been feeling every day since it happened. Let's face it; I left my dead sister's children with her crazy husband Jack. Deranged Jack."

Carla nods in sympathy. "You had no choice, with Jack the Ripper as the middleman. And you were 3000 miles away. How could you possibly prevent what happened?" She puts her head on my shoulder, still hugging my sleeve. "You loved your sister. Charlie. She will always be with you."

We sit there and gaze out to sea. I think about why I very much appreciate her friendship. I remember our drive to Big Sur last summer with our friends Rose and Laury. Laury was driving. Carla sat in the back seat with Rose. I was in the passenger seat. We were off to a 10K team relay run to support Breast Cancer research. It was only a couple of months before Priscilla's death. I was happy that day; just having personally raised almost $1500 through donations; anticipating a wonderful time that day - until I threw up!

The car started twisting, turning sharply on the cliff roads. Cliff after crazy cliff. More cliffs. I didn't even think of this before I agreed to do this race. Heights frighten me. Sharp cliff edges drive me insane. Pure, miserable panic. I don't know why I react this way. I clutched the sides of my seat with quiet but fierce intensity; pressing my lead-heavy legs into the floor mats - wishing I could brake and stop the fucking car; exit the torture chamber. "Turn around," I remember silently screaming inside my head.

Laury was driving the car, humming to the radio tune. She didn't notice me sweating, freaking out right beside her. Embarrassed, I closed my eyes, trying to fake a nap. I could feel my face clenching up. My grip on the seat getting tighter and tighter. My eyes wouldn't stay closed with my nerves so frazzled. I grabbed a tissue from my purse to wipe off the sweat. It was pouring out from my temples. Carla was in the back seat to my left. I could feel her gaze on me and then I heard her speak emphatically to Laury.

"Take the next turn off Laury. I need to get out for a minute."

Laury lowered the music. "What? We're going to be late Carla. We've got exactly thirty minutes before the relay race starts. We've got to get signed in and set up as a team. We'll be there soon. Trust me. No worries."

Carla persisted. "Laury, just stop the car at the next turnout. It's urgent!"

Oh shit! The steepest cliff I've ever seen was now on my right; my hand desperately holding onto the armrest. Laury shrugged her shoulders and turned off at a sign which read 'Vista Point.' Relieved, I pushed open the car door as soon as we stopped. Laury jumped out to let Carla climb out of the back seat.

Carla rushed over to me. "Sweetie, are you ok? I could see how green you looked. You were sweating up there. Clenched up tight." Carla took my hands to comfort me. "Oh god, your palms are sweaty too. You poor thing. What's going on with you?"

11

Weakly, I managed to speak. "Damn it, it's those cliffs. I just can't take it. I like the edge, just not cliff edges." I felt sick to my stomach. My head was reeling. Laury and Rose looked perplexed and then agreed to split an energy bar. I threw up in a bush on scenic Vista Point. Carla held my damp, clumped up hair, as I pathetically puked.

Carla took further command and announced, "I'm driving the car now. I know what to do, how to take it slow and careful. Charlie's having a rough go with these cliffs."

Laury reluctantly handed the keys to Carla. "That's fine Ms. Andretti. I will now hand over the car keys to mild-mannered Carla Lopez," Laury said sarcastically. "Let's just get there," she added; annoyed. Carla, always looking out for me. Carla, like the sister I couldn't be to Priscilla. Carla, like the supporter I can never become for Priscilla. Suicidal Priscilla. Gone.

I come back to the present, here at Rio Del Mar beach with Carla. "Why didn't I pay attention to the clues? Poor Priscilla. Her depression was extreme. I have a Master's in Psych for Christ sakes. I should have jumped on a plane as soon as I realized the depth of her depression. I dropped the big sister ball." Carla breaks in. "I know it's hard for you Charlie. But Priscilla is gone and you are here - alive, healthy and successful. Everything to live for. With you here and Pris in Florida - you couldn't possibly give her the help she needed."

Tears spill down my cheeks. Carla grabs the empty doggie poop bag tied to Sadie's unoccupied leash and with it, attempts to wipe away my tears. We catch each other's eye in that moment, empty poop bag wiping up my tears. We burst out giggling. It's our standard pattern. Painful moment; and then sudden shared goofy laughter. I'm thankful to break through this sudden dismal mood. The dogs rush up to us. We hug them and playfully wrestle them in the sand. Their tongues are thick with saliva from racing the beach, dribbling all over us. I spring some treats from my vest pocket and offer them to hyped up Sadie and Clyde.

I spring up with brightened energy. "No more tears," I say. "Let's run back with the dogs. I'll race ya." Carla smirks at my idea. Her competitive spirit kicks in.

"Okay, Ms. Perky Pants. This time, for a change, I'll beat you. Last one to touch the Rio Beach sign eats the rest of the doggie treats in your pocket. Deal?" Carla inquires, raising her eyebrows and bearing a sarcastic grin. I take the remainder of the treats from my pocket to show the ante. "You maniac! Ok. Deal! On your mark, get set, Go!" We race back.

Carla yells out, coming up right behind me, as we approach the beach sign finish line. "Olé, olé, olé, olé, she sings out musically. Hey Perky Pants, I hear blondes have more fun than anyone in Havana. Getting my groove back, I win the race. I wonder, did she just let me win? I watch her eat two doggie treats.

Chapter Three

EXIT CALIFORNIA TO MEXICO

Doug escorts me to the security gate line at SFO. We get closer to our impending point of goodbye. I get ready for the security routine, as I start to remove my belt and shoes – feet now completely exposed on this filthy floor. The joys of travel. I think they recently just started doing the shoe removal thing. It bugs me.

"How are you going to carry all that stuff? Doug asks. "Maybe you should have just packed one big suitcase instead of all these small carry ons." Doug - my reliable advisor.

I respond, "I'll be fine. No worries. You know me, world traveler. I'm used to this." Doug pulls me to him and places a long soft good-bye kiss on my lips. His kaleidoscopic blue-green eyes stare into mine.

"I'm going to worry about you pumpkin. Be careful, to say the least. Think of me; especially when you're dancing around, kicking your heels up." He touches my hair and smiles. "Can't wait to see my kids in Maui, but you will be on my mind all the time." His eyes narrow. "Damn it Charlie, I'll be worried sick about you."

Suddenly, I'm feeling a bit guilty, leaving this caring man at holiday time. But if I'm honest with myself, I can't wait to get on that plane to start my adventure. Sometimes, I wish I felt more passionate about Doug, matching the intensity he seems to have for me. He's a high quality guy.

Doug nuzzles my ear and whispers, "Imagine just you, me and the Hawaiian trade winds. Sound inviting?"

I inquire, "Did you say you're staying in Lahaina through next Friday with Monica and the kids?" It was bothering me. "Doug, I didn't realize that."

He rushes to answer. His defensiveness surfaces. "Yep, that's the plan – then I'll move up north to the Napili beach condo and wait for you; probably have the kids spend a few days with me there before your arrival."

I kiss him on the cheek and whisper. "Okay honey, but be a good boy, hmm?" He shoots me a sheepish grin and nods as I release from his embrace. The thought of his ex-wife's potential reaction to the idea of Doug and I living together crosses my mind. She will probably freak out when she hears about this; if he tells her.

Show my passport to the first security check and then scooting down the line, I grab a few gray plastic bins for my belongings. I make long distance eye contact with Doug as I scramble down the security line, my plastic bins jerkily passing through the hand baggage screening tunnel.

"Good-bye Doug." I gesture with a wave as I pick up my things on the other side of the security gate. I watch him as he walks away. He's gone.

"Mexicana Airlines, Flight 430 to Cancun; now boarding at Gate 15. We are ready to board first class, 1K and business class passengers at this time." Shit, that's my flight. The loudspeaker announcer beckons me to race away from Starbucks, where I must get a latte or I'll fade away. I haven't had my coffee yet. It takes forever for the young European twenty something in front of me to get his unfamiliar American money out of his duffel bag. He finally pays the cashier. All he gets from Starbucks is a bottle of water. Yes, hard to believe. I add sweetener to my skinny vanilla latte at the condiments counter and re-gather all my crap, quickly turning, ready to dash to gate 15. Geez, I'm only at gate 7. I crash head-on into a large man. My stuff scatters to the ground. My heavy backpack now hangs uncomfortably. I'm stressed. I bend down. The backpack drops to the floor with a thud, painfully yanking my back. The stranger kneels in front of me. His eyes are huge dark orbs and his hair is black as black gets, and falls fully around his manly neck.

He speaks with a pronounced accent. "It's a good thing I have the medical insurance," he says. "If I'm going to suffer physical damage, this would be, how you say, the ideal way to get injured?" He smiles. His teeth are not perfect but they align very nicely with his crooked, warm, genuine smile.

I'm discombobulated. I explode with an apology, "I am so sorry. Please, don't worry I-I can get these things myself. I need to rush. Sorry." I say it again." He picks up my back pack and then my camera bag, easily juggling his own carry-on with my things.

"What gate? What gate are you going?" His accent is Hispanic, I'm sure.

"Uh, gate 15." I'm now holding my boarding pass which I have just retrieved from the grubby airport carpet.

"A heavenly coincidence," he struggles to get this last word out in clear English. "Me too, gate 15. Si, this is great. I can help you with your things." He smiles. "I will carry your back pack. Let's go."

Perplexed and thankful, I silently agree. We walk fast. "It appears that you brought a bag of bricks with you, yes? Going to Cancun to build a new mega hotel with your load of bricks?" he questions playfully. I smile and nod. "Heavy, huh? I've got a lot of odds and ends in there; all part of my camera equipment. Sorry." I apologize yet again.

Another announcement blares out, requesting everyone to board immediately through for Cancun.

"I am Enrique. Enrique Ruiz," he says in raised voice, as it's getting noisier in the departure lounge area; dozens of people rushing to line up for the now boarding Gate 15 flight.

He speaks in my ear as he follows close behind me. "I am on my way to see my family in Habana, Cuba; going to Cancun for a short holiday first."

I almost erupt with: "Oh my God," but I resist the urge. He pronounced it Habana, not Havana, I think to myself. I like that. I show my boarding pass to the flight attendant. The woman takes it, smiles and rips off a segment; returning half back to me. Enrique Ruiz, I think he said is his name.

I turn around as I move through the gangway tunnel to board the plane, and say, "I'm Charlotte Sweeney. Friends call me Charlie. Good to meet you Enrique. Shall I take my stuff now?"

He shakes his head. "No problem. I will put these in the overhead bin for you, si?" His thick dark eyebrows question me to confirm my agreement.

"Great, thank you again Enrique." I appreciate it. Just having left Doug only some minutes ago, I'm feeling suddenly a bit disloyal. I look at what's left of my boarding pass. I'm in row 20, aisle seat. I crave the aisle seat any time I fly. I get claustrophobic, don't like to be hemmed in the middle seat or scrunched in by the window seat; and then there's my issue of heights.

"What row are you sitting?" he asks in his somewhat broken English.

"20," I say.

"Good, I am only a few rows behind you." He lifts my back pack and shoots it right into the overhead bin above me as I sit down.

"Until landing, señora. A pleasure to meet you." He almost bows for crap sake.

I drop into my seat; dazed. He's going to Cancun and then to Havana. Ayiyiyiyiyi. Do I tell him my plan? Why would I do that? I probably won't even talk to him after this flight. I'm very logical. Thinking, always thinking. I get up to let a mother and daughter pass to sit next to me. Cute little girl. Her pigtails swing from side to side as she scoots into the seat with her Dora The Explorer mini back pack. She's maybe six or seven years old. Dimples. Red hair. During the flight, I play a series of Fruit Ninja games with the giggly little red-haired girl. Her name is Emily. The flight is pleasant - uneventful; until the last

15 minutes. Rocky air pockets. The drops suddenly. It's a roller coaster ride here in the sky. I grip my seat armrests the whole time during the final descent; trying to mask my fear to the other passengers around me. But I think the little girl knows what's going on.

My eyes close, attempting to mentally disconnect from the current scene. What a chicken I am. I'm feeling totally out of control; wishing that man, Enrique Ruiz was by my side with his charming Latino accent – distracting me from my thoughts of doom. I think to myself, what a freaky woman I am. I'm daring in so many ways. I love racing cars, going really fast on the freeways and back roads; often getting into some trouble with the highway patrol. Most of the time I talk my way out of a ticket; once, even when I was wearing a nightgown. Here I am freaked out, landing on a safe runway in a regularly inspected American passenger jet. But, I'm cringing as we hit the ground hard on landing. I notice other people laughing. A few clap their hands.

"Thank you for flying United. We know you have a choice of airlines. We appreciate you choosing us. Have a wonderful time in Cancun," the pilot announces in a deep southern accent. Once we taxi to the gate and hear the familiar cabin chimes, everyone instantly disengages their seatbelts and stands up, ready to get their belongings and speedily exit the plane. Enrique comes to my rescue yet again; retrieving my back pack from the overhead as I grab my camera bag and loaded purse.

"I'll just take it out to the luggage claim area for you and you can go from there. You have other luggage? I'm guessing, yes." He looks down at me with a bit of a saucy grin. He's tall; I think maybe 6'2". I consider how old he might be. I wonder if he's older or younger than my 38 years.

"Oh, yes, thanks so much. So nice of you," I reply.   I'm singing inside with delight and at the same time, feeling slightly awkward with his chivalrous behavior. Hey, I'm just making travel friends as I go along, I say to myself. No harm done to anyone. No harm at all.

Once I get my luggage, Enrique almost gives me another even more formal bow, bending forward from his upper body. Nice upper body, I think.

"So, Miss Charlie Sweeney. Did I say your name right?"

"Hmm hmm. Perfectly."

"Bien. I guess you are going now to your hotel. Would you and your friends like to have dinner with me at my cousin's Mexican restaurant here in Cancun?

Caught offguard, my mind races, and I fumble my words. "Uh, well, I'm actually on my own in my hotel. I-I'm just spending a few nights here on a mini holiday." I nervously stammer this out. I can see he's a bit taken aback, but quickly recovers.

"Ahh, well then, you cannot decline. You could meet me at the restaurant. It's called *'Hacienda'*, very close to all the major hotels, and with a beautiful vista. Your hotel is which one? he inquires.

"Uh, the Royal Solaris Cancun. I think it's only about 15 minutes from this airport."

"Maravilloso Señora," he says with his Latin flair. As we exit the terminal and move to the taxi stand, Enrique tells me more about the restaurant.

"The Hacienda is only about five minutes from your hotel; a very short taxi ride. And, taxi drivers know this great restaurant very well. I will meet you there at 6:30 p.m. Yes? A friendly dinner and you can meet amazing Miguel, the owner and head chef. He is my cousin."

"Okay. I'll be there," I agree. A taxi driver rushes over to pick up my bags.

"Adios then Charlie - for now. I notice the slight indents in his cheeks; almost dimples. "See you tonight." He waves his hand, and I wonder what he's thinking as my taxi driver swerves into the lane of honking, screeching cars - fighting to get out first.

Chapter Four

CANCUN — FIRST VIVID MOMENTS

Shades of turquoise and navy blue ocean 180 degrees - the view from my second floor balcony. It's breathtaking, and the image below at the hotel pool and on the beach resemble a Bruegel painting. There are small scenes happening everywhere I look. I take in a myriad of vignettes, one after the other. A spirited group of twenty-somethings are having drinks, probably mai tais, and laughing as they float lazily atop pumped up plastic rafts in the water. Happy people, old and young, are boarding the catamaran on the sand for an afternoon sail. Dozens of children scream as they gleefully glide down the twisting waterslide at the hotel pool. As each child hits the water, their siblings and instant hotel buddies wail with laughter. I zero in on another scene; a young mother at the poolside with her toddler situated just above the shallow end, right below my window. She crouches down and bastes the child with large quantities of sunscreen that she applies from a tube she retrieves from the edge of her lounge chair. The baby cries and fidgets disdainfully. The mother whispers in the baby girl's ear. The result is a series of instant giggles from the youngster. I can't hear those giggles, but I visibly see her explode with laughter. I wonder what the mother said to change her mood in just a quick moment. The mother scoops up the child in her arms, hugging her while carefully descending the short steps leading into the pool. Mom is adept at responding to the needs of her little daughter. I notice this. I grab my camera from my bag in the room, quickly attaching the long telephoto lens. Rushing out to the balcony eagerly ready to capture the cute, gleeful look on the child's face. I aim my Nikon for the shot. But the mother and child have vanished. How did they disappear so quickly? I search the canvas of activity below. I don't see them anywhere. I hate to miss shots like that.

Disappointed, I lay down on the blue-striped cushioned lounger on my half-shaded balcony. I'm feeling sleepy. My head is reeling with thoughts of Havana; already getting a little nervous – anticipating my next steps in the coming days. Do I tell Enrique? I drift into a REM state; half asleep, half awake.

My mind conjures up a dismal scene from my past. There is no dialogue in this scene. We are at my sister's gravesite. My brother Sam stands with me. I am weeping, tears falling down my cheeks, holding onto Sam, my brother who is "alive." My sister Priscilla is dead. The burial scene plays out in my head; in slow motion. I throw a long stem red rose on the fresh grave. As I turn my head to my right, I see Jack – my sister's husband. He looks vacant and mean, holding the screaming baby, his two young sons by his side – both dressed in tight under-sized, dirty white shirts and crooked skinny black ties. Jack's three unkempt and fat Southern bully brothers also stand there with their stoic expressions – their faces like stone statues, as if bodyguards for Jack, who seems to be uncomfortable. He stares out beyond me into the distance; and appears "alone", although flanked by his various family members. He shakes his head back and forth, back and forth. Instead of sadness over the death of his wife, he resembles an angry pitbull.

Tanya, the baby girl, fidgets in his arms; pushing Jack away with her strong chubby little hands. The only sound I can hear in this scene is Tanya, starting to cry; louder and louder, until she is screaming at the top of her little lungs. Pushing, pushing her hands and feet into her father's chest. Fighting him. He grabs her arms sternly and smacks her little hands, roughly scolding her; then glares down into her innocent eyes, giving her a stern warning. Still no sound in the dream, except for Tanya's screaming. He shakes her. I see him roll his eyes, making eye contact with his largest Mississippi brother whose shirt is riding up, exposing his pale, hairy skin; pants falling down below his grotesquely fat stomach. Is that a gun in his jeans pocket? My eye zooms in on his right front pocket. The outline seems to form the shape of a small pistol. Thugs, I think to myself. He notices me look over at him, and as if on cue, spits out something gross onto the ground. It looks like chewing tobacco. I turn away in disgust. I'm shaking. My brother, Sam, notices too, and squeezes my hand.

I throw the second rose onto Pris' grave. The baby continues to scream. Then – another sound. It's a pounding heart beat taking over my dream. It gets louder and louder. Is it you Priscilla? Is that your beating, yet breaking heart? Then I hear her voice. "Charlie, Charlie, I didn't do it to hurt you. The end looked better than the future. The end looked better than the future," she repeats.

I awake with a start. It's the hotel phone blaring out an old-fashioned telephone ring. I stumble into the room from the balcony, half groggy to answer it.

"Hola, little girl. In your bikini yet - fooling your comrade turistas with your fake Cancun party persona?" It's Carla. I am grateful to hear her voice.

"I have someone here who wants to talk to you," she says. A loud sniffing sound comes through the earpiece, then heavy dog-like breathing. It's Clyde.

"Yuck. Stop licking my phone you silly mongrel," Carla playfully scolds Clyde. "Hey Sadie, it's not time for you to copy Clyde's slimy behaviors. Those two!" she exclaims. "Sadie does something, then Clyde copies it. Then Clyde does something, Sadie copies that. Lovebirds," she sings into the phone. "Romance is certainly heating up around here. I can see the way he checks out Sadie. I think he's forgotten about his missing master, or is that mistress?"

I smile into the phone, now fully letting go of my bad dreams.

Carla continues, "Oh and by the way, I just got a call from your babbling beau, Doug. Yep, he called to say he was concerned and wanted to know my opinion on your trek to Cuba. In a back-handed way I think he was sort of chiding me about having encouraged you to make this particular journey.

I respond, "No kidding? I think Doug is just concerned about me. I can't believe he's already called you to check in. I don't think my cell phone is working here in Mexico. Probably tried to reach me and no joy. I thought that might happen. I'm so happy you called Carla. I- uh-well, I had a strange thing happen, actually."

"Already? she questions. "It's only been one day, if that. You haven't decided to run away and become a snorkel guide in Cancun, have you?"

I sigh, thinking, should I even mention Enrique Ruiz to Carla? Yes, she is my best friend. "Well, I met this man in the airport. His name is Enrique. He's Cuban. He's on his way to Havana with a stopover here in Cancun to see his cousin, who owns a popular local restaurant."

For some reason, Carla doesn't offer her usual quick retort. For a moment – total silence. I wonder if we're disconnected. Finally, she speaks. "Really? That's interesting. Well, just enjoy him. Totally let go, my friend!"

I quickly add, "Oh, it's nothing – no big deal. We were just on the same plane from SFO, and…."

Carla breaks in, "Oh shit, I've got to go now. Lance, my new winter romance is coming over for dinner and the oven just beeped. The pork loin needs more basting. I still have to shower and put on my slinky little black velvet dress. Get the make-up on. Keep up the mystique. So, be safe best friend. And enjoy your few days in Cancun. I'll let Doug know that I spoke to you, and that you are fine - indeed. Of course, no mention of the hunky stranger. Tee hee," she wickedly teases me.

"Ok Carla, I already miss you. Give Clyde a smooch for me. No tongue alright?" I tease her back. "Bye for now."

Two hours later, after I'm more than decently cleaned up, I take the elevator down to the spacious hotel lobby. It's bustling with people of all age groups - coming and going. I hadn't noticed the splendor of the immense lobby when I first arrived, probably because I was still reeling from the Cuban Enrique Ruiz. Standing outside the hotel entrance in the tropical early evening, the hotel attendant opens the taxi door for me.

"Señora, you are going where tonight? "

"The Hacienda Restaurant," I reply.

"Bueno. Me gusta. You will love the vista as well as the food. For the main dish, I advise the garlic-lime shrimp. Bueno, bueno."

"Gracias," I struggle to get out the Spanish word, and then feeling more confident, I add, "Gracias to you señor."

He gives me a wink, and shuts the taxi door just after he shouts out to the taxi driver, "Hacienda, por favor."

As we drive away, I'm trembling a bit. Why? I reconsider my choice of outfits for tonight. I know that I got some sun on the balcony this afternoon and I'm already looking brown in such a short time. I'm wearing my indigo blue paisley strapless halter dress. "Is this the right look for a friendly date?" My hair is shining; recently highlighted, courtesy of the gifted and versatile Carla Lopez. I can see myself in the driver's rearview mirror. Yes, I am feeling good tonight; completely carefree – no big business, no Doug, no dog to walk, no pressures at all. Then I feel my nerves perk up again. I admit it. I am somewhat jittery about tonight. I still haven't decided on exactly how much to share with Enrique about my life; especially about my Havana destination. "Anyway, it's not a date. Is it a date? No, I think to myself...*not* a date!"

Once the taxi stops at our destination, I can see the gorgeous ocean view through the majestic entrance - which features two huge consecutive white stone arches. These structures are flanked on each side with elegant signage which simply states in traditional script: "Hacienda." As I walk through this arched gateway, I see several tables situated on the perimeter of a spacious open air balcony which is adorned with tiny soft blue lights strewn magically across the deck. The lights twinkle brilliantly as the late afternoon sun hits them. The giant burnt orange ball begins its spectacular setting on the royal blue ocean. Mexican music plays in the background.

I see two men chatting at the bar, which is situated adjacent to the dining area full of navy blue clothed-covered tables. It's Enrique. He is talking passionately to a tall, large, rather corpulent Mexican man.

The other man has a mustache, a thick mass of dark, dark hair above his lip. He has a bit of a roughshod appearance but wears an immaculate white apron over his loose- fitting black long-sleeved shirt and baggy pants; finished with a red starched bandana tied around his hefty neck. He looks strong. Then, there is Enrique, who immediately notices my entrance. As he rises from his stool and gestures to me to join them, I see that he looks incredibly handsome tonight. Yes, Enrique is a stunning man; dressed in a crisp black aloha shirt which is covered with small muted green palm trees. His simple black jeans hug his lower body. Nice fit, I think.

The scene is an echo of my first gaze at Enrique Ruiz at the SFO, just after I slammed into him. Both times, he's managed to take my breath away. As I approach the restaurant bar, I can see Enrique's eyes up close and personal; large deep dark brown saucers, almost matched to his dark shirt. His hair is just the right amount of ruffled; those thick waves of black. For the first time, I notice the sprinkling of salt and pepper at his temples. I glance at his hands. No ring. Whew – thank you God. I failed to check that earlier. Why does that matter? I think this to myself. Shit... I can't help but be attracted to this man. There is a part of me that wants to run away right now; take back my entrance, take back the deliberate swing of my long blonde hair as I make my way to the bar; secretly wanting to entice this man. Geez, I need to calm down. Now!

"Charlie, or should I introduce you as Charlotte?" He graciously asks me with a slight rasp in his deep Latino voice.

"Call me Charlie. That's fine," I say. I almost gush when Enrique speaks my name, but catching myself, I straighten up; determined to offer back a classy greeting. Damn, I'm tingling with excitement no matter what I do or think. He can probably read this.

Enrique smiles and says, "I am happy for you to meet my favorite cousin, Miguel - owner and head chef of The Hacienda."

I hold my hand out to shake Miguel's hand. Instead, Miguel grabs me with a quick, but all-encompassing bear hug. I didn't see that coming. He is part gentle and part brutish, all at the same time. It's as if he's trying not to reveal his intense physical strength, as he embraces me.

"C-cousin," he stumbles slightly on this word. "How did you find this beautiful woman?"

I can feel my face turn red. I am, of course, flattered. "You keep your hands off this lovely new friend of mine," Enrique breaks in. He jokingly punches Miguel, putting up his hands as if they were covered with imaginary boxing gloves. Hmm, he's already a hero to me.

"Let me seat you and get you settled." Miguel guides us to the dining room. "I have reserved the best table for you, at the corner of the patio, looking out to the ocean."

Miguel leaves us to take in the scenery.

We sit at our table and gaze out at the spectacular vista. Enrique talks a little about his mother in Cuba. He is happy to be making the journey to see her as it's been almost four years since they were last together. Enrique asks me why I am here alone in Cancun. This is the second time this topic has arisen in the dialogue between us. I explain that I have such a heavy work schedule. "Now that I have a break with the time off, I thought I'd just hop down to Cancun for a personal holiday – to decompress." I also add, "I'm an amateur photographer. I was thinking that Cancun would be a good place to capture the colors and faces of Mexico."

Enrique nods in understanding, then responds, "Yes, Cancun. It is a colorful place. There is no question. But - there are so many other places where the people and culture are even more interesting. Belize and Argentina or even Brazil; and of course, other more remote parts of Mexico, In those places, you can find charming tucked-away villages and towns that are not focused on just selling to the turistas. Here, in Cancun, most everything is tourism, tourism, tourism." He chuckles at himself.

I am thinking the same thoughts but purposely not sharing. Should I give away that the only reason I am here in Cancun is because it is a fairly convenient gateway to Cuba? I'm still not convinced I should open up on this point.

Enrique continues. "Things tend to feel fake in Cancun; everything manufactured for the masses. Okay not everything – but mostly everything. Getting outside Cancun is much better. Bueno! Bueno! Ahh, but this sunset is magnifico, isn't it?"

"Yes, it's enchanting here tonight," I agree, smiling. Mexican cantina music plays in the background – now even louder as the sky darkens. "The music, do you like it Enrique?"

"Sí, sí. Mexican music is okay. You know, in my country there are many things I don't like, it's true; but the music is not one of these things. Cuban music is hot, sultry and mucho rhythmic. You cannot help but dance when you hear it. Your heart begins to beat with it. Cuba! Si, a place of heartache and limitations in terms of personal freedoms. But without any doubt, the people and culture are irresistible. I am happy to be going for a visit, though it will be brief."

We sit together for a few minutes just staring silently out at the ocean. I feel comfortable in this silence between us. Usually with Doug or with Carla, or even with Sam, there is always talking; continuous chatter. Sharing this verbal pause with another person is refreshing to me. Gives us time to quietly appreciate the night, our surroundings, this incredible view; just experi-ence it - without words. I'm loving this.

Complete darkness takes over the tropical night sky. The tiny blue Hacienda Restaurant lights hanging across the balcony cre-ate a soft mood, a serene atmosphere. The lights swing gently in the light wind. I can feel Enrique's warm gaze on me.

Miguel approaches our table, singing the Mexican melody to the background music. He greets us again. "Cousin, you would not believe the noise in my house these days. Three small boys and a new bambino. This is why I come here to my lovely restaurant - to get away and have some peace. Sonia wants to see you, Enrique. Stuck in the house with those little ones, she doesn't see many men." Miguel winks. "Other than my boys, there are women everywhere at home. Too many sister-in-laws. I barely get to say anything in my own house." He guffaws with deep laughter at his own joke and continues, "I'd ask you to come over tonight, but how could you tear yourself away from this attractive señora?

"Si, Si Miguel," Enrique agrees with a nod. "I will come by tomorrow morning and stay for the day. I have some American gifts for the little ones, and something very special for Sonia." Now it's Enrique who gives Miguel a wink.

Miguel pretends outrage and grabs Enrique's arm with some force. His face takes on a confrontational expression.

"They are kidding, right?" I think this to myself. Miguel's muscles bulge out, as his black shirt sleeves are now rolled up and hugging his upper arms.

"Hey amigo, I do not share my woman. Comprendes?" Enrique says with manufactured aggression.

It must be a male thing. Hmm - a little macho, I can't help but critique this in my head. The two men ring out with shared laughter and again, mime the imaginary boxing thing.

Enrique's voice suddenly changes from a frivolous mocking tone to a more serious, tender one. "Cousin, look out into the sky. What do you see?"

Miguel, still half laughing and appearing surprised, says "stars, a small moon, ocean, but it's dark now – not much to see."

Enrique disagrees, shaking his head. "No Miguel, there's plenty to see. How about that twinkling star? Look, it's just beginning to do its nightly dance and shine for all of Mexico to see." Enrique points, putting his right forefinger up to his eye and with his left hand he gently pulls his cousin Miguel down close to his face. With silent animation, Enrique encourages Miguel to look straight up at the biggest and brightest star we can see. Miguel's huge body is now bent down, with his eyes intently following Enrique's forefinger pointing up to the sky.

Enrique smiles and almost whispers, "That star is like your Sonia. The most brilliant diamond in the sky is just like your wife. You are one lucky man Miguel. I am humbly envious. You have the love of a beautiful woman who has given you four spirited niños." Miguel nods and raises his eyebrows in agreement. "Your blood line will go on for at least another 100 years and maybe more. Yes, a lucky man you are."

Miguel appears moved by his cousin's uninhibited expression of emotion. At that moment, I can see how intimate these cousins are with each other.

"Enrique Ruiz seems too good to be true," I think to myself. Life is good. Then a question enters my mind. Why is this man single – not taken? Or, is he taken? I wonder.

Miguel breaks the tender mood and says brightly: "Well Enrique, I will see you tomorrow. Sonia and the boys will be pleased that you can spend time. Please excuse me. I need to get home. I am already late leaving. I am sending over my best waiter. Carlos," he yells. "He will take good care of you."

"Muchos gracias Cousin." Enrique responds. "See you mañana - about 10 o'clock. Sí?"

Miguel looks pleased, adding one more thing, before he departs. "By the way, I recommend the garlic shrimp. It is done in a lime, cilantro reduction. In fact, it is the signature dish of

Sonia and these days, the most popular plate at my Hacienda Restaurant."

Both Enrique and I stand up to say goodbye as Miguel, once again bear hugs me and this time, gives me an even more robust squeeze. "A pleasure to meet you, señora. I hope we see one another again."

As he disappears into the bustling kitchen, Enrique smiles, inviting me to sit back down. He is charming. The candle on the table now casts a shadow across his face, highlighting his distinct features. Strong square jaw, high cheekbones, huge eyes and again that kind of crooked half smile.

"Miguel," Enrique says, "my special cousin Miguel. I love him. He came from Cuba eight years ago – managed to get out and re-start his life here in Mexico. And Dios mio, he has built this wonderful, most popular restaurant in a new country." Enrique is beaming with pride for his cousin. "Now, my lovely new friend Charlie, let us eat."

Carlos, the waiter is now poised with a pad at our table, ready to take our order. Staring at the menu in the candlelight, almost at the same time, we look up at Carlos and both say "garlic shrimp." We start to giggle at this synchronicity. The meal decision is made. Enrique orders a pitcher of Sangria plus some guacamole and warm, tasty house- made chips to start. I am delighted with everything so far tonight; the food *and* the company I'm keeping.

The fruity Sangria wine hits the spot. Not my first rodeo with good Mexican food and Sangria. A pitcher of this delicious reddish, purple drink is full of floating bananas, orange slices and cherries. Combined with the best and maybe only garlic-lime grilled shrimp I've ever tasted – this meal has me singing with satisfaction. As the mariachi band appears suddenly at our table, I am already humming the familiar tune.

"Guantanamera! Enrique, I love this song." I am gazing now at that brightest and largest star, I see "Sonia," as tagged earlier by Enrique, and I smile. He notices me looking up at the night sky.

The mariachis approach us and zealously sing out, " "Yo soy un hombre sincero, de donde crece la palma. Y antes de morirme quiero."

Enrique reaches across the small blue clothed-covered table and touches my hand. In a hushed voice, he translates the Spanish phrases, "I am a truthful man, from where the palm tree grows. And before dying I want to let out the verses of my soul. Beautiful woman of Guantanamera." He stops; his eyes looking down at my hands.

Consider me enchanted now. The mariachis sing the song impeccably, with exquisite harmony. As the tune ends, Enrique stands up and stuffs some money into one of the mariachi's vest pockets. "Gracias amigos," he says with great relish. "Bueno, bueno."

Enrique talks about the music. "Guantanamera, this is actually a Cuban song. Did you know that Charlie?"

"No, I didn't really know the song's cultural derivation," I respond.

"Yes," he continues, "there are actually two versions as to what the lyric is about. One version is about a man, un hombre, who falls in love with a woman from Guantanamera. They have a heated, long and intense love affair. Finally, she leaves him for a secret reason – we don't know why; never to be seen again. Now, the other version is that this woman he has fallen in love with does not love him back, has no romantic relationship with him; although he is completely mesmerized by her beauty. For her, it is merely, how you say, platonic?" He pauses. "Fascinating, Sí? I am full of useless musical facts."

His dark twinkling eyes peer deeply into mine. I'm getting used to the endearing slant of his mouth when he's amused. I fidget a bit awkwardly in my chair. Enrique gestures to one of the mariachis to please visit our table. The most elaborately dressed mariachi happily approaches. Enrique gets up to whisper something in his ear. The band of guitarists start to play my most favorite of Mexican mariachi songs. The familiar instrumental lead-in to the song tells me that it is indeed Besame Mucho. How did Enrique come up with that song? I know that it's popular and well-known; but it feels like such a serendipity. I remember that Besamé Mucho is about kissing, a lot of kissing. I can feel my face heat up, and not as a result of the sun on my balcony this afternoon. I am blatantly blushing at this point.

Enrique takes my hand and lifts me gracefully from my chair. "Let's dance."

He escorts me to the open area of the patio floor between the decorative carved wood bar and the dinner tables. "I will whisper the translation in your ear," he says, "if you don't mind. Si?" He smiles down at me, looking for my affirmation. I am a little taller tonight, probably 5'6" instead of my barefooted 5'4".

I nod and say, "Yes. I will follow your lead." I feel his hand touch my lower back as he leads me in this dance. He moves with flair, rhythmically; his hips seem to naturally swing to the beat.

"Bésame mucho, bésame mucho," they strum and sing.

Enrique begins his English version in my left ear, speaking softly, on the fringe of actually singing the words. "Kiss me, kiss me a lot, as if tonight were the last time. Kiss me, kiss me, for I am afraid to lose you; to lose you after this." Enrique gently glides me across the wooden deck. Although not a formal dance floor, another couple, young and very tan – maybe on their honeymoon, move from their table to join us. They smile with appreciation at our bold initiative. Other dining couples observe us, looking envious, but without the nerve to take to the floor.

The mariachis play on, gaining momentum as the beautiful song continues. Enrique's moves get slower, and now gets even closer to me; his hips still swaying to the music. I can feel his strong body against mine. He doesn't press hard, but I make out each individual muscle in his body. He continues to translate. As the song progresses, his moves get even slower. His voice starts to fade. Then, I feel him tense up a bit as he turns his head slightly away from me; almost hiding his face. I suddenly feel a spot of wetness fall onto my bare shoulder. "Is he sweating?" I wonder. Another drop falls, and slides just a bit down my back before soaking into my skin. It's not very hot tonight. A light breeze sweeps across the patio from the ocean.

As the song ends, Enrique stops dancing and takes my hand, whispering in my ear, "Come with me, I want to show you something." I'm feeling a bit confused. He was so anxious to dance. What's going on now?

He carefully guides me up a spiral wooden staircase located adjacent to the bar, which opens, after two dozen or so steps to another upstairs patio. We are directly above the main restaurant. This patio is plainly decorated and features another sprawling sculpted wood bar. It's quiet on this other open air level tonight. Nobody is here but us. The wind blows a little harder than on the downstairs level; but it still feels warm and pleasant. Enrique takes me to the edge of the balcony. It's a good thing for that it's completely dark now. I can't tell how high we are or if there is a steep cliff just below. It's okay; I feel safe with this man.

"Charlie," he speaks in a low register. "I am so sorry Charlie. As you say in America, "I *lost it a little bit* while we were dancing. I was thinking of someone gone from my life some time ago. She is no longer of this earth." He hangs his head. "You must have noticed my mood change while dancing." I stand beside Enrique and find myself lost for words. "Please accept my apology," he continues.

Now I realize that my shoulder was dampened by his tears. I am speechless. I place my hand on his as he holds onto the iron railing, which hangs out over the ocean.

"It's okay Enrique," I whisper. "I understand loss. Don't worry. No need to apologize. I am not at all insulted."

He looks up at the black sky, gazing directly at that one bright shining star. He speaks with a weak and almost philosophical tone.

"That star, it reminds me not only of Sonia; but also of this woman I used to be very close to personally. Her name was Rita."

For the second or third time tonight, there is a long, yet comfortable silence between us as we look out at the white-capped waves riding the violet sea; lit up from the restaurant spotlights below us. The crescent moon, visible earlier, has disappeared behind some clouds. The sea seems to be getting rougher, matching our mood of inner turmoil. I am still grappling with grief; much like this man.

My thoughts travel far away from this balcony here in Mexico; and for a moment, I think of Priscilla. She is my brightest shining star but no longer shining. Priscilla, my baby sister, five years younger than me. Four years younger than Sam. Priscilla, who finally became my friend as we grew into adulthood. As kids, my brother and I constantly teased Priscilla, calling her a baby on a daily basis. We even nicknamed her "little field rat" and created an accompanying dance a la Soupy Sales; used often when she invaded our almost twin-like collective space. Sam and I were only eleven months apart. I remember another childhood song we used to tease Priscilla with, where we once again replaced part of the lyric with our own customized wording. "With a knickknack tally whack, give the dog a bone, Pris, the field rat comes rolling home. Pris, the field rat comes rolling home." We would sing out, screaming as our lungs would allow, so the other neighborhood children would hear us. We sang it over and over, and often; making Pris cry time after time. She would go running to our spaced-out mommy for support. Sam and I had no patience for her kid sister questions; questions we had answered for ourselves years before. We could be cruel to our sister.

Our family of four lived out of one small bedroom in my grandmother's apartment in the Bronx – our obsessive compulsive mother, me, Sam and Priscilla. The females slept in one queen bed, my brother in a small cot near the window. My grandmother slept on her roll-out couch in the living room. I think it was a Castro convertible. The place was infested with cockroaches and waterbugs. We were petrified every day.

Enrique breaks my dismal yet reminiscent train of thought. I come back to the present. I am grateful to him. I love hearing his voice. "What is happening to me with this man? Forgive me Doug," I think to myself.

Enrique gently pulls me close to him. "Charlie, let's turn this sullen mood around. I really don't mean to be, how you say, gloomy; on such a wonderful night. Tomorrow, I am with Miguel and his family, as you know. But the following day, if okay with you, I would like to take you to Isla de Mujeres – a stunning island habitat full of Mexican sea turtles. I promise you a day of sun, sea, - the simplicity of nature and the enjoyment of a wonderful little village. Please say yes." The sound of his invitation is divine.

I nod and say, "I would love that. Thank you. I'll take my camera with me and shoot the turtles. You know." I grin. "I meant *photograph the turtles*, not literally shoot them. Sí?" I giggle looking at the visible confusion. I almost levitate above the wooden deck, I am so stoked.

"I hope you enjoyed our dinner - in spite of my sudden sorrow. I will call you a taxi now to take you back to your hotel." He is so polite.

I nod; but stop him as he starts to move down the spiral staircase. "Wait," I say, "before we end tonight, I'd like to share something with you about my trip."

He stops, looks into my eyes and senses my slight hesitation to speak further. I proceed to confess. "Um – well Enrique, I'm actually on my way to Havana."

He tilts his head and gives me a quizzical look. "Habana, my home? You are going to Habana? But why?"

"I know it's a bit risky, but it's a dream I've had for a long time. I want to see Cuba, experience Havana. I understand it's somewhat illegal for U.S. citizens."

"One question - do you have a special visa?" he asks.

"No, I don't. I believe it takes months to get one. But -but, I have a good plan."

"Ah, really. I see." He rolls his eyes in jest.

"I'm an amateur photographer. I've traveled the world doing portrait photography. He listens intently. "Yes, it's a hobby. I've captured the diversity of different cultures across the world. A few of my photographs have even been published in a couple of magazines."

He touches my hand, following my words carefully. I continue. "I want to reflect the emotions of the Cubans, capture your culture with candid portraits of the people."

Enrique seems intrigued, flashing me his warm smile. He puts his forefinger to his lips, pondering my now exposed plan. His eyes then seem to light up in the dark on this windy Mexican patio. He shakes his head and chuckles. "Charlie Sweeney, you amaze me. You are full of surprises. First Cancun, same destination as Enrique. And now, Habana – also same destination as Enrique. I guess I am a very lucky man; not only my cousin Miguel, eh?"

Back in my hotel room, I open the balcony door - enjoying the night, now alone and content to reflect on my first day in Mexico. It was the evening agenda that makes my slightly sunburned skin tingle, thinking about Enrique. Although he has already shared so much of his personal and intimate thoughts, I still feel that he is a big mystery to me. I don't even know what he does for a living. It's funny, I didn't even think to ask him nor did he question me on this topic. Usually, the first thing to share with a new acquaintance is your occupation; but not in our case. For us, the usual chit-chat fell by the wayside.

A contrasting thought floats across my mind – Doug. I should at least try to text him. I grab my cell phone. Shit – I forgot to charge it; now, for almost two days. Oh good – it's still got some juice left. Damn, it's not working right. Maybe I should call him from the hotel room phone. Maybe not, I decide. I vacillate back and forth. I'm tired. I can do that tomorrow at a more reasonable hour. I still have two more nights here – my last chance to connect with him before I take off for Havana; or should I say Habana a la Enrique's pronunciation? And tomorrow, I will be hanging out on my own, so there will be plenty of time.

Anyway, I wouldn't know what to say to Doug right now. The tone of my voice might tip off that I'm feeling much more than physical distance from him here in Mexico. A blanket of depression now falls over me. I feel like I've cheated on him despite nothing really happening physically with Enrique; nothing I'm ashamed of at this point. I feel really lonely right now. The crescent moon has appeared again in the night sky. The clouds have passed and the sea is calm. The sound of the waves soothes me as I ready myself for bed.

Chapter Five

PRISCILLA — MY LOST SISTER

I lay down on the cushy down pillows in my hotel room. Nice crisp sheets too, cool to the touch. I am still feeling low. Closing my eyes, I see a giant blue crystal, turning red then back to blue, then to violet, and then back to blue again. The crystal lifts my mood. Clarity of thought jumps in. If truth be told, I am feeling guilty. Guilty about Priscilla, guilty about he knee- jerk feelings growing inside me for a strange man I just met, and in fact, met through an accidental collision. "Am I on a collision course? Was that symbolic?"

I have two dreams tonight. The first dream repeats an actual Florida scene from a year and 12 days ago. It was the day before Priscilla's funeral. My beautiful sister was dead. My brother Sam and I had taken both Kevin, 6 years old, and Brian, only 4 years old to Cocoa Beach We wanted to some how comfort my dead sister's two boys. Reluctantly, Jack had finally caved in and agreed to let us out the door with his two boys; the two year old baby Tanya staying back with Jack. Before he agreed, I could see him on the edge of violence with his youngest boy, Brian, who was craving constant attention from his father. Brian was hurting and still puzzled by the sudden and total absence of his mother. Jack seemed annoyed, becoming more agitated by the minute with both of his sons that morning.

"Yeh, okay, get them out of my hair," he spoke gruffly to me. He gave us an approved window of exactly two hours for this beach excursion. "That's it," he muttered. Be back by 1 p.m. – no later. Ya got it?"

We quickly organized the boys with light jackets as we rushed out before Jack had the opportunity to rescind his decision. My dream then morphs into the beach scene with the boys. We sit in the sand, the two youngsters, me and my brother Sam. The boys are automatically drawn to digging with their hands, grabbing chunks of wet clumps of sand and throwing them in the ocean. I make designs in the sand with a long stick. My brother glumly stares out on the vast blue ocean. Clouds threaten rain; but the sea is calm. Kevin starts to throw fists of sand at his little brother. I think back to what Sam and I used to do to Priscilla when we were kids. I quickly go to Kevin and Brian to intervene. Brian is getting hit right in the face with heavy wet chunks of sand. As I approach, Kevin, the elder picks up a handful of wet sand and throws it right in my face. Anger and aggression pour out of his little body. Shocked and feeling the harsh sting in my eyes, I fall down. Kevin, surprised that he hit me right in my eyes, instantly drops to his knees crying uncontrollably. I brush myself off, try to focus my eyes and quickly go to him. I hug him. He struggles, not wanting to be touched, but then gives in, falling limply to the sand. I embrace him; my arms around him.

Through his sniffles, he cries, "My mom – she's gone. She's dead! Dead! I saw her face in the car, in the garage. Dead – hunched over the steering wheel. I thought she was sleeping, but she was dead! Fuck. Fuck everyone. My mom – I want her back." He screams, beating his fists into the wet sand. I try to cradle him like a small baby. He tries to reject me again; pushing me away. Then, collapses in my arms like a lifeless doll. I feel Sam watching us from a distance as he walks quietly over to Brian, who is busy digging in the sand, oblivious to his brother's outburst or to me. Sam intentionally prevents any interruption between Kevin and his Aunt Charlie.

I am dazed; my eyes are still stinging. I hear myself say to Kevin, "It's okay sweetie. Your mom is still with you in spirit. She is like the gentle wind we feel right now. Do you feel it?"

I sit up on my knees in the damp sand and show Kevin that I am feeling the breeze and can sense his mother watching over him. "She's touching us, hugging us in her new way. Do you feel that soft breeze?" He looks at me as if I'm an alien from outer space. Then he sits up on his knees, next to me. He closes his eyes to feel the breeze. There is silence.

After almost a full minute, he says, "Yeh, okay - I feel it. But it's not mom."

I look down at him with my open heart, questioning him and urging him to re-consider, without me saying a word.

He closes his eyes again to feel the wind. He opens them, looks up at me and admits, "Maybe it is mom. Do you really think she's with me - still?"

I ponder his innocent question. "Yes, I feel that she's at peace now. And - she's watching over us. She wants us to live on and even be happy. Maybe it will take awhile for us to smile again, but she's asking us to carry on and do good in the world."

"Yeh," he says, "she was always crying and scared at the end. I felt bad for her. I would yell and scream mean things at her sometimes, make her even sadder. Then she would just go and cry some more in the bedroom. I felt bad; but I still did it. I made her mad. Now she's dead." He drops his head in shame.

I hug him yet again with all my might. "I understand, I understand. But it wasn't your fault," I say softly.

Kevin and I draw hearts in the sand with our sticks for the rest of our time at the beach. Kevin writes: "Mom I love you," inside two of his biggest hearts. We watch the tide start to come in, erasing the hearts we've meticulously drawn. Then we create some more hearts further away from the waterline. Hearts that still remain as we leave the beach.

I awake from the dream. The red LED display of the clock catches my eye. It's 2:35 a.m. For a moment, I forget where I am. I am wet with sweat. I change pillows, grabbing another and try to fall back to sleep. My second dream tonight is at my sister's house again in Florida. It's a few hours after the morning funeral. Our flight is late afternoon from Orlando. We have quite a drive to get there. We notice that it's starting to rain, as Sam and I exit Priscilla's house, probably for the last time. Jack is once again flanked by his three husky brothers. Sam and I are preparing to leave in our black rental car. There's no audible sound in this second dream until the very end. It is all played out in mime; only actions and movements. Jack is holding his baby daughter as he stands at the open front door. The brothers escorts us using non-verbal belligerence. I sense their intimidating physical aggression; simmering just below the surface. I notice the outline of the pistol in the fat one's jean pocket.

Kevin and Brian look on from behind Jack; still inside the house. Kevin breaks through the physical blockade and runs to me. He grabs my arm, indicating that he doesn't want me to leave. The baby girl fidgets in Jack's arms. She stretches out her chubby hands and legs, determined to get down. Jack roughly pulls her back towards him, smacking her infant arms with his large hand. With his other hand, he yanks Kevin away from me.

There is sound from this point on in the dream. "Go to your room Kevin Lee. Now!" Jack commands. "It's time for them to go. They were only here for a short time to see your mom get buried. You know that kid. Now – go!"

Kevin hesitates. I can see him deciding whether to defy his father. Jack clenches his fist and raises his hand, threatening Kevin. This gets Kevin's attention and he heads towards his bedroom, looking back at me with his large green eyes, again, silently begging me not to leave him - not to abandon him.

The baby starts screaming. Her cries get louder and louder. Then – a lone heartbeat takes over my dream. First low, then loud, and then deafening screams. My body jerks in the hotel bed. I'm falling, falling, falling into a large sea of blue crystals. They seem to have sharp edges but they are still beautiful, reflecting magically off one another. It's stunning and frightening at the same time. I fall onto an expansive, shimmering bed of royal blue crystals. I startle, awake, recalling the two dreams; each one having accurately depicted some of my most intense real-life experiences over the last year; all except for the crystals. Where did the crystals come from? What do they mean?

I glance over at the clock sitting by my bed. Wow. Already 10:05 am. The two dreams continue to race through my mind, in rapid playback motion. Priscilla, I will never know exactly what was the last straw which catapulted you over life's fragile edge. I attempt to erase these painful scenes from my consciousness, with little success.

Chapter Six

CANCUN — MAKING NEW FRIENDS

I decide to try my cell phone again in the hope of now connecting with Doug. I'm feeling overcome with obligation. Suddenly, I realize that I failed to call the damn cell phone company to have them arrange for the phone to work outside the U.S. Consciously, I had not called them as I knew that eventually I'd be getting to Cuba and didn't want to be tracked. Of course, I wasn't planning to make any calls from Cuba. Geez, I guess I can't use my cell. Calling Doug from the hotel phone would be pretty pricey. I can afford it. Perhaps I'm just being passive aggressive. In truth, I don't really want to be voice to voice with Doug right now. I lay there paralyzed with my dilemma. For a second time in 24 hours, I decide not to phone Doug. I know that he's leaving for Maui today. Probably occupied with getting to the airport, etc. etc.

Soon, he'll be completely occupied by his still jealous and dependent ex-wife, Monica; and re-united with his two kids. Monica continues to hate me, having incorrectly assessed that Doug and I were sexually involved well before their marital split. It's not true. I had held back both physically and romantically until their separation was a reality, a done deal. Anyway, I think, Carla has already soothed Doug's concerns. I laugh to myself. In Carla's own way, hopefully she has quelled his fears for my safety. Oh Carla, you brat. I can just imagine what you said to Doug and how it came across.

Chortles of laughter from the kids at the hotel pool rise up and through my open balcony door. I peek over the balcony, still in my long pink cotton nightie, to catch a glimpse of the activity around the resort. It is another glorious and sunny day in Cancun. The gentle Mexican instrumentals play out from the audio speakers in the pool area. The only negative in this tableau is now suddenly coming from the patio restaurant just below; adjacent to the pool area. A loud series of screeches invades my ear space. Tables are being moved on the patio floor by a group of Mexican hotel workers. The high pitched sounds block out any sound of the once pleasant background music and obliterates the voices of the tourists enjoying their vacation at The Royal Solaris. The ear-wrangling high-pitched sounds echo throughout the expansive resort. The irritating noise seems to surprise a bunch of people who are in and around the pool. They quickly cease their hearty activities in search of the source of the problem. As soon as they realize what it is, the various groups of vacationers resume their activities, seeming to ignore the raucous racket; though honestly, the sound seems to be getting worse.

They must be closing up the morning breakfast buffet and getting ready for lunch, completely re-arranging tables. I notice how people just adapt to their changing environment, even when there is an unnerving and intrusive disturbance. The table dragging continues for several minutes. That must have been one hefty buffet, I think. Funny – how I continue to be offended by this obnoxious and piercing cacophony. Hotel management should be able to find a more elegant process; especially if this is happening each and every morning. Maybe put some attractive rubber matting under the entire table area. Just do something about the problem, I think to myself. Good service is important to me; always has been. Finding creative and practical solutions to those pesky business and customer problems is critical; especially when it spoils the enjoyment of the resort guests.

For a moment, I feel like quickly slipping on my clothes, rushing downstairs to find the resort manager and giving him or her my customer relations advice. Normally, I might even do just that. But this time, I decide, instead, to just "chill out". Finally, the noise stops. Everything is back to normal – no more screeching!

I pick up the leather bound binder titled: *Your Royal Solaris Resort Guide.* I'm in the mood to just hang out today close to the hotel; not do anything significant. A good time to bask in the sun and float in the pool. Maybe have a nice Mexican breakfast and take a walk. I wish that the next 24 hours would fast forward, so that tomorrow could arrive instantly - my day alone with the most attractive man I've seen in Mexico so far - Enrique.

I satisfy my morning hunger with the huevos rancheros special. As I request a second cup of coffee, I ask my waiter about the local marketplace. They are unbelievable treasure chests for photographers; overflowing with candid expressions from both vendors and patrons; intense activity everywhere. The local color and culture jump out in spontaneous shots caught and "frozen in time". I crave the market hub bub – babies, children, adults and elders mingled, jumbled altogether. Often families of two or three generations work markets. That's how I remember it in Tblisi, Leningrad, New Delhi, Bangkok – some of the most interesting portrait photography locations I've encountered.

I'm not sure if Cancun will live up to my best shoots. But I'm hopeful. I walk only three blocks from the hotel and I am at the marketplace. Colorful Mexican goods available in dozens and dozens of stalls – fruits, vegetables, knick knacks, purses, shawls, kitchen gadgets, towels – you name it. I find myself shooting a family of tourists from India. I ask one of the female adults wearing a sari if it is okay for me to photograph them as they experience the market. She nods and smiles, flattered at my interest in her family. The little Indian girl, probably about 6 years old, speaks to me. Her English is impeccable. The faces of her family members are enchanting, each unique, captivating, especially in the midst of a Mexican marketplace. The girl introduces herself as Sunita and her mother, Balvinder and then her Grandmother Suri. "Oh and that's my brother Pritpal, over there. "We are from Bombay. We used to live in London." Sunita says. I wind up shopping with them, buying a few cotton embroidered tops for myself and one for Carla. Balvinder has a good eye for quality and beauty when assessing the goods for sale. I continue shooting them with my camera, capturing their interactions with vendors and their delight and occasional disdain with the various items. They seem to have a lot of dialogue between them when considering a purchase. This makes for good photography. Sometimes, I shoot them from afar; several stalls away. For me, it's zoom lens heaven.

The Indian family decide to leave the marketplace at the same time as I do. I thank them for their willingness to allow me to enjoy their adventure at the market through my photography. We say our goodbyes. Yet, they seem to walk my same route back to the Royal Solaris Hotel. The little girl rushes up from behind to catch up to me.

"Are you at the Royal Solaris?" she asks.

"Yep, I am."

Her eyes widen happily. "Will you go to the pool today then?"

"Yes," I say. "Actually, I've been thinking about jumping into the water as soon as possible. I'm so sticky from all that shopping. You too?" I ask.

"That's great," she replies and claps at the same time. "My great grandfather is waiting for us at the hotel. He will join us at the pool. He says he has a surprise that he can't wait to share. I don't know what it is." Her eyes widen with excitement. She skips along beside me as I continue to walk at a good clip.

"Are you curious like me?" she inquires.

I laugh at this rambunctious little girl. I love young children. Raw feelings, emotions, open and honest thoughts – all day, every day. "Well, sure, I'm always interested when someone has a surprise secret that they are about to share, I half whisper to her in confidence.

"Then, you must come," she says. "We are first stopping for Grandmother's coffee, so I will see you there. We will be at the shallow end - for my brother," she says, a little bothered. "I can swim in the 9 foot deep end by myself - no floaties needed. I'm really good. You'll see."

She waves goodbye and skips back to her family still somewhere behind us. It's funny to me that this whole family from Bombay, India, has chosen Cancun for a family vacation.

Entering the hotel pool area about an hour later, the suns feels hot. Immediately, I spot little Sunita. As I walk towards the family who are spread out across at least five lounge chairs, I notice the addition of an older Indian man. He must be the grandfather. Little Sunita eyes me and charges over, very excited. Her missing front tooth adds to her charm.

"Is that nice looking man your grandfather?" I tease her a little. She giggles.

"Really, he is my great grandfather, 80 years old," she emphasizes the number. I can hardly believe it. He looks fit, but now closer, I see his many deep wrinkles and age markings. Still - he looks very healthy. "His name is Great Grandpapa Gurjot. He is a very wise man, a yogi and the smartest in our whole family,"

Sunita beams with pride. Balvinder, Sunita's mom, welcomes me to their lounge chair camp and has graciously saved an empty lounger for me. The pool area is bustling, every chair occupied. I am touched that Balvinder has thought of me.

"This is my great grandpapa Gurjot." Sunita introduces us. He holds out his long skinny aged-spot marked hand. I can feel his yogish wisdom and his power coming through his grip. His eyes are light brown pools of kindness. He has a gleaming set of teeth for an elderly man, large pure white pearls.

"A pleasure to meet you," he says. "Sunita has told me about your photography at the marketplace today. She is asking me to buy her a really good camera for her upcoming birthday." He rubs his chin in mock thought and looks down at his great grandchild. "Hmm, I don't know. Maybe," he shakes his head playfully back and forth." They all laugh.

Balvinder breaks in. "You are too generous Papaji. Don't rush and buy this child an expensive camera. Forget about that for now, what about your own 80 year birthday surprise?"

"Ahh yes," he says. Okay - all of you, come over here," he gestures to the whole family clan. They rush over to his lounger; as I do as well. "Look, you see that man in the sky." They all automatically, as if choreographed, look up, but they seem puzzled by this start to his surprise. "That man, flying – he is parasailing. Today is my birthday – right? They all nod in unison, their eyes getting larger and larger as they listen intently. "What if your great Grandpapa decided to do such a thing? Would it be okay?" He waits for their reaction.

Balvinder grabs the back of his lounger, almost falling to the ground. "What are you saying? It's a joke, right?" she pats his upper shoulder.

"No, I am scheduled to do this thing at 2 p.m. today. I am doing it!" he exclaims.

Balvinder is mortified. The kids giggle. Grandmother Suri shakes her head as if she already lost a battle, giving up. Personally, I am amused by this old man. Is he kidding or what? With my fear of heights kicking hard into my brain, I am almost frozen in silence.

He looks up at me, "So what do you think, am I crazy? Would you do it?" I'm still frozen.

"Would I do it – me?" I ask myself. Then I answer him. "No – no, I don't think so. It's much too terrifying for me. I confess Great Grandpapa Gurjot. I am dreadfully afraid of heights – very much a scaredy cat, as we say in the states."

"No, you are a brave one. I can tell." He announces this with great conviction. "What if you come with me, and overcome your fear of heights problem? Face it like an angry dog." He makes a fierce expression. Then he softens, "Brave one, let me ask you differently. Would you please accompany me parasailing and make this 80 year old man's birthday forever memorable?" He pleads with his big dark, almost large eyes.

I don't know what in the world overtakes me at that moment. It's the way he said, "You are a brave one." I gulp, and say, "If you really want me to do it. I don't want you to have to go alone."

Still staring deep into my eyes, he nods emphatically. What the hell am I doing? But the words tumble out of me, as if I have no control. I just automatically respond. "Yes, then I will go with you Great Grandpapa Gurjot."

The kids clap loudly in delight. Balvinder appears to be a bit relieved for some reason, now that I've agreed to do this insane thing too, with her grandfather. She looks at him and still tries to reason with him. "Grandpapa, please don't be so foolish. It is nice that this woman has actually agreed to accompany you; but I don't think this is wise for a man of your age. Forgive me, but I know it is your choice; but I am very afraid for you."

He stares caringly at her for a moment and considers her plea. He looks over at me. "Charlie, you will definitely join me then? No turning back once you give me your final agreement, yes?" I can't believe it's me talking.

"Uh, y-yes, okay, I will do it." I still cannot believe that I am saying yes to this old man's provocative request. As if hypnotized, I'm under his spell. But I trust him, much like I've begun to trust Enrique.

We take a little boat out to a large wooden platform a good distance from shore; just far enough to be concerned if you had to swim back to land. Our Mexican guide is in his early 20's; fit, rugged and seems to speak almost no English. I'm wondering how he will train us on what to do when strapped to the parasail, how he will give instructions we will need to be effective on take off and landing; and especially on how to stay safe. The guide rips the boat across the water at breakneck speed. I notice that Great Grandpapa Gurjot is looking lean and frail with his shirt off, clad with only a life vest hugging his bare upper body in preparation for the parasail. His bathing trunks are short, exposing his bony legs. I'm getting worried. My brief confidence at the pool when I agreed to this hair-raising stunt has now gone sailing out to sea. When we reach the wooden platform,

I say: "Great Grandpapa Gurjot – will you go first?" It's only us out there on the platform.

He tone turns serious, "Charlie, there is one important thing to remember from this point on." I'm expecting a statement of wisdom from this man whom I've come to quickly respect.

"What is that?" I ask anticipating an even more provacative request from him. Instead, he shoots me his million dollar smile and says, "Yes, what's important is that from this point on you call me just *'Gurjot.'* The *'great grandpapa' title* is not necessary. I cannot help but smile. He has thrown me off guard in his own adorable fashion.

"Okay, *Gurjot,* I will watch you go first."

"No, no," he commands. "*I* will be the one to watch you. It is the brave one who will take the first ride. I will observe you and learn from your bravery."

Annoyed, I say sharply, "Why should I go first? I know nothing about parasailing. Nothing! And I'm petrified, Gurjot!" I almost begin to sob. Again, that savvy smile sweeps across his weathered face.

"Well young Charlie," he says as he shakes his head back and forth, "I want to see what happens. If you don't make it, then I know it's time to thank my lucky stars, forget about this ridiculous endeavor – and have our guide return me swiftly back to shore, unharmed." I stare with intensity at Gurjot, taking in his words. I'm confused. Then I just burst out laughing. He got me again! This old man gets such pleasure in teasing me. We both laugh uncontrollably – one 80 year old kid from India and one 38 year old American kid. Definitely – two zany youngsters, getting into trouble. Big trouble.

Our parasailing guide glares at us to straighten up, breaking our silly laughter, gesturing in question, "Who will go first?" I feel like pointing at Gurjot but think better of it. I raise my hand, obeying my elder, as he shoots me a stern, yet encouraging look.

Shit, I think, am I really doing this? Have I gone insane, literally over the edge? The guide harnesses me, with his rough and dirty hands, pulling at the contraption he puts me in and then laying out the attached parachute behind me on the platform. The chute actually looks beautiful, though a bit faded from the sun. I can see some of it with my peripheral vision. Climbing back into his tiny boat, he puts his thumb up high to indicate we are going now, and to get ready. He turns back making eye contact for me to nod okay. Gurjot stands to the side behind me, out of the way.

Gurjot yells something. I say, "What?" The guide revs the motor and takes off. Suddenly I jolt and I am up in the air.

Gurjot is cheering from down below. "Charlie, the brave one has taken off!" he yells. "Charlie, the brave one is flying high!" I can hear him clearly. He's almost musical. He yells it again. "Charlie, the brave one is flying high!"

The speed of the boat increases and now I'm pulled way up into the air. My fear of heights begins to take control of my psyche. I'm panicking; probably turning bright red. I start to sweat. But surprisingly, my panic seems to subside when I take the time to look around and survey my surroundings. I can't help but focus on the vibrant colors, the unforgettable vista, the beauty of height. Yes, the beauty of height! This phrase resonates in my mind. A totally foreign thought for Charlie Sweeney. Height – I'm now internalizing that it may not be the enemy.

The ocean boasts at least ten fervent shades of blue and green. I notice this palette of incredible colors as we coast along the shore and then out into the sea, and back again. Stunning! The air is refreshing, smooth and energizes me. I know it is the hottest part of the Mexican day, but I feel pleasantly cool. I am cool, I chuckle to myself. Oh shit, I am really high. I yell out, "hooray," probably nobody hearing me from way up here as we are now far from Gurjot and the platform. Maybe the guide driving the boat hears me. This is awesome! If I had a chocolate mint ice cream sundae right now, then I'd be in absolute and total heaven. Before I even have time to take it all in, I'm slowly descending. We move first right along the shoreline full of sunbathers and ocean dippers, then into the final descent flight path, and back to the floating wooden platform. I quickly land the chute without thinking, touching down on the deck with my bare feet; then stopping like Stravinsky's firebird – with a good degree of grace and artistry. I thoroughly impress myself.

Gurjot is laughing, applauding and singing in delight. "The brave one is back! The brave one is back!"

Quickly the guide releases me from the harness and places Gurjot in the same contraption. He rises up in the air – looking frail and very small. The harness is overwhelming, swallowing his body. I look up. Wait! He is holding up a sign. Gurjot rolls out a scroll of some sort. As he unfurls it, I see the whole thing. Written in big fat black letters scripted in a beautiful form of calligraphy, the sign reads: *"80 YEARS OLD AND CRAZY!!!* Some people swimming on the beach point up to the sky, and seem to enjoy this hilarious messaging. I can hear their collective cheers. More and more people continue to shout as if they are watching an Olympic athlete achieve greatness. Minutes later, the amused Mexican guide shakes our hand as he delivers us safely to shore in his little boat. He appears totally jazzed as we have successfully managed to create major publicity for him on this beach.

We jump out of the boat. Gurjot seems to reel just a bit. I help him back up the beach where his entire Indian family greets us, screaming out words of joy.

"We saw you – both of you. You are so brave." Sunita yells to us. Both Pritpal and Sunita jump up and down with excitement.

"Yes, brave and crazy," Balvinder chimes in. She is smiling too, and does a quick visual once over to check out Gurjot's physical condition. Suri, the great grandma just shakes her head back and forth, but this time she wears an approving smile. Back at the pool, the hotel has actually arranged a cake for Gurjot congratulating him on his birthday and his achievement out there. There is bustling all around the lounge chairs. Birthday singing and 'For He's A Jolly Good Fellow' is sung by a group of tourists, who evidently thoroughly enjoyed Gurjot's show as well as a little more than tipsy from their margaritas.

Gurjot looks over at me, through the crowd of celebrators; his bright eyes shining. He winks and beckons me to him. He hands me his black lettered sign. "For you, brave one. Keep this to remember what you did today and who you did it with."

I beam with pride in our partnership and my sincere appreciation for his steady encouragement. Charlie Sweeney – forever brave from this day forward, I think to myself. I nonchalantly flip over the sign. On the other side, it's written: **_"CHARLIE - THE BRAVE ONE!"_** Wow. I thank him with my eye contact and smile as Sunita pulls me into the pool for a swim.

After about an hour of swimming and pool play, my head remains up in the air – still parasailing. Time for me to be alone to reflect on this insane day. Saying a final thank you to Gurjot is not enough but I can see he knows how much I treasure today's experience. As Sunita pulls out a sheet of paper and a pen to have me write down my email address, Gurjot reaches into his madras-print satchel which rests on his beach towel. He sits up cross-legged on his lounger and hands me a small object which is wrapped in a deep blue velvet cloth.

"Shh," he puts with his fingers to his lips, requesting me to keep this transaction a secret." I comply and quickly stash it in my beach bag. I write down my email address, and give Sunita a big squeeze goodbye. She reminds me that the whole family is leaving on a plane tonight to L.A.; then onto Bombay. As I bid farewell, this time it's me giving Gurjot a bear hug. Did I learn this from Miguel? I think of Enrique. I miss him. I can't wait to see him again – to share today's adventure. Perhaps my achievement today is no big deal to most of the world - but for me, it's a momentous accomplishment.

Walking away from the Singh family, and now in the hotel elevator, I open the dark velvet cloth which reveals a good-sized bright blue, beautifully shaped crystal. Seeing it takes me back to my dream – the bed of crystals which I fell into just before I awoke this morning. It makes me think of magic! Magic can happen instantly without any foreshadowing, I think about this as I marvel at the mystic object in my hand. Maybe it is magical; like that wise old yogi, Gurjot. I place the object safely away in the pocket of my camera bag.

Chapter Seven

ENRIQUE — THE MYSTIQUE

Back in my room, my entire being is still energized from my demonstrated bravery. Famished, I order room service. A chicken quesadilla with the extra addition of hot jalapenos. I adore them – the hotter the better. I am informed that dinner will arrive at my door in about 50 minutes. The kitchen is busy tonight. After a quick shower, I put on my Royal Solaris complimentary white robe and walk out onto the balcony; fully refreshed. Sunita and her family have disappeared from the pool area. Their previously occupied loungers appear untouched, as if not a soul sat there today. I visually scan the resort. Nope, they're gone; most likely busy preparing for their late flight tonight. My eyes wander to the beach area and pause to look at a familiar figure. At least the man looks just like Enrique from here; same physique, same wavy dark hair, same height. I can't make out his face very well in the shadows of the late afternoon; his body half hidden by a large beach umbrella. He's talking to a guy wearing a uniform, looks like a hotel waiter. This man wears dark-rimmed eye glasses, has some sort of goatee and long black hair tied back in a short ponytail. Their heads are close together, as if talking in hushed tones. The sun is close to setting and the scene from my balcony gets dimmer and dimmer. I'm sure that's Enrique. I think he's wearing the shirt he wore on our journey from San

Francisco – a striped aloha shirt. I see the uniformed man walk away. Enrique now stands alone, staring out to the ocean.

I quickly dart from the balcony into the room to once again grab my Nikon to zoom in on this scene. I zoom in. He's gone. The spot where he stood is empty. Why would he be here tonight? I know that he said he's picking me up tomorrow in the lobby at 9 am. Looks like I'm having an on-going problem losing new friends whenever I go for my camera. I chuckle to myself and at the same time, an edgy, uncomfortable feeling overtakes me. Maybe I'm just so smitten with this new man in my life that I'm starting to see him; even when he's not there. Scarey.

The phone rings. "Charlie, it's me - Enrique." His voice is serious and indicates concern. "So – you are really still there at your hotel? I thought maybe you left Mexico already. I called your room three times today to check on how you are settling in at the Royal Solaris." Catching himself, he takes on a lighter tone. "Tell me, are you having a good time on your mini holiday in Cancun?"

His voice excites me. "Sí, Sí Enrique, I'm having such a great time. I've been out most of the day making some *other* new friends." I tease him a little.

"Ah," he replies. "I thought maybe my behavior last night may have scared you all the way back to California. I thought you were gone Charlie. It was, how you say, 'disconcerting' for me."

I adopt a mock commanding voice. "Señor Ruiz, you underestimate my resilience. You must think that you have great powers of influence, enough to drive me out of this country, and back home. What delusions you have amigo."

He chuckles. "Tell me how does one influence the independent, sassy and may I add, very attractive Charlotte Sweeney?"

I giggle with slight embarrassment. My face heats up and I see crimson cheeks looking back at me in the mirror. "Where are you now Enrique?"

I'm just about to inquire on whether that was him on the beach awhile ago, when he replies, "I am just lazy, sitting here on Miguel's back deck, smoking a Havana cigar, thinking of our time together tomorrow. By the way, are you planning on leaving the day after tomorrow with me to you know where?" He whispers this last sentence into the phone. "I can help guide you safely to your destination."

I take in his offer and I realize that, as yet, I hadn't thought about the specific logistical details of my exit from Cancun to Havana, either with Enrique or on my own. I didn't, however, anticipate that our departure time would exactly coincide. On the other hand, maybe that would be ideal – leaving at the same time and on the same flight, accompanied by someone familiar with Havana.

My mind races to the big elephant in the room. He said he's at Miguel's house right now. I guess that wasn't him on the beach then. Does he have a twin brother? I consider asking about this, for a second.

"Are you okay Charlie? He breaks the silence. I must have paused a bit too long, with my thinking and processing of his new information. He fills the verbal void. "Not to worry Charlie – we will talk tomorrow. Just know that I am willing and able to help you depart Cancun with a smooth transition to Habana. No passport stamping and cash only, which you know is the strong recommendation for U.S. citizens with no pre-approved visa."

"Yes, I am nervous about my entry," I admit to him. "I would really benefit from your knowledge and support. Thank you Enrique." I am feeling somewhat reluctant to talk more about Cuba on the phone. My paranoia cracks the surface.

Changing the subject, I say - more upbeat, "I'm looking forward to our day at, I'm sorry - is it Isla Mujeres? Is that what you called it?" I'm sure that I'm butchering the place's name with my awkward mispronunciation.

"Sí, our beautiful destination in the morning, Isla Mujeres."

Hey, I got it right. I silently applaud myself.

He continues. "Si, be sure to bring a change of clothes Charlie and beach gear, of course. Bueno. Mañana then - beautiful lady." He's closing our conversation.

"Enrique, remind me to tell you the details about the special time I had today."

"I cannot wait," he says. "No, truly Charlie, I mean it. I can't wait to see you again. You have been on my mind all day long; even here, playing with Miguel's children and visiting with his wife. I miss you Charlie. I cannot deny this."

I am more than a little pleased to hear him say those romantic words. "Good night, Enrique." I'm smitten. He whispers softly into the phone, "Señora, buenas noches." Then he hangs up. Whatever that was at the end of his call, I liked it. I liked it mucho mucho.

A knock at my hotel door. I hope it's my food. I am now officially starved for my chicken quesadilla and guacamole. I look through the peephole. A short, skinny waiter is standing there. Opening the door, I realize that this man resembles the man I thought I saw Enrique talking to on the beach earlier. He wears the same hotel uniform; and his slight build, his goatee, his glasses and his ponytail look identical to that man. This is definitely the waiter from the beachfront, but was he talking to a different tall man? I guess – it wasn't Enrique. Anyway, why would Enrique be here at the Royal Solaris, when he said he's at Miguel's? What reason would he possibly have to invent such a story? I almost drum up the guts to inquire with this waiter who doesn't say much and honestly doesn't appear to speak nor quite understand English. He keeps smiling but without eye contact as he arranges the food on the roll-in table. I say nothing to him about the scene on the beach. He leaves. I eat everything in sight. The jalopenos are hot, hot, hot. I forgot to order anything to drink with dinner. Despite this, I resist drinking the tap water and I'm too lazy to go down to the lobby and grab a bottled water. I'm in Mexico. I go to sleep thirsty.

Waking to tables screeching across the restaurant patio below, I look at the clock which reads 7:45 a.m. I am refreshed. No dreams last night – no reminiscences of my dead sister, and even without a glass or two of wine. Not bad. Bueno! I'm deep in the latin mood after only two days in Mexico. Shit, I forgot to try to call Doug yesterday, too; caught up in the glow of my astounding parasailing feat. Maybe I'll call him tonight.

At 9 a.m., after I grab a bottle of water and a pastry, I show up outside the hotel lobby to meet Enrique. That must be his vehicle. I'm looking at a shiny black Jeep Cherokee adorned with beautiful italicized gold lettering splashed across the passenger door car door panel, which reads: *Hacienda – A Restaurant for Love!* This wording also features those two exquisite white stone arches. A matching logo appears on the back window. The SUV is parked by the valet desk but nobody seems to be inside. Suddenly, I feel something touch my upper back. I reflexively jump. Turning sharply, I see its Enrique.

"Hey you," I lighten up, and give him a playful punch on his arm.

"I surprised you, Sí? Sorry if I scared you. I didn't think. "Loca cabeza. Loca cabeza." He knocks his fist on his head in faux punishment.

"I'll live, you brute. Let's go!" I take his arm and he beams at me with pleasure. He plays smooth Latin music as we embark on our drive to the harbor where we will catch the ferry to Isla Mujeres. On the road, I am feeling excited and anticipating the experience of yet another new place. My Nikon sits on my lap, ready for anything.

We arrive at the ferry harbor, just five minutes before launch; barely time to get our tickets and board. The ferry takes only 45 minutes; and then we are there. Immediately, I am turned on by this environment. Tropical, yes, and almost poetic with vivid color. I glide down the boat ramp and almost trip, falling into Enrique's arms. He's saves me once again.

"You're beginning to remind me of Dudley Do Right," I burst out giggling.

"Dudley who? Qué?" he asks.

"Oh, Dudley, he's an American cartoon hero. He's constantly saving some damsel in distress – just like you do!"

" Yes, but I am real, not a cartoon - and gestures of your personal appreciation are gratefully accepted any time and every time." We seem to have a comfortable and wonderful tete a tete going between us, I think to myself. I could get used to this.

Enrique gives me some background on Isla Mujeres; which, he is Spanish for Island of Women and is one of the ten principalities of the Mexican state of Quintana Roo. Hmm, I wonder how many other women Enrique has introduced to this heavenly paradise. He continues to explain that the island is actually only 8 miles from Cancun and just 41/2 miles long. Lush, lush, lush. I am delighted when Enrique escorts me to the moped scooter counter adjacent to the ferry landing. He requests two mopeds, letting me know that the transportation on this island consists of only taxis, golf carts or moped scooters.

"No problem, I'm up for some scooter time. The last time on a scooter was on the island of Mykonos in Greece. I hope I remember how to drive one of these things," I add.

We jump on the scooters. I have my beach pack secured on my back. I am ready. Enrique leads the way around several twisting bends, each exposing sweeping views of the ocean. We arrive at a place on the water. It's a sea turtle farm. We swim in the blue green waters and observe a variety of large, multi-colored sea turtles, with their orange and white underbodies and green backs, with speckled heads. I shoot numerous photos from the water's edge. These creatures are amazing to watch, gracefully skirting through the water; their short functional legs flapping with ease. Enrique is careful not to touch them, but to point our the beautiful spots visible on their broad backs, as we swim around for the afternoon. We dry off and embark on a tour through the turtle farm, listening to the guide describe the turtle's mating season – referring to the female turtles as "the lovely ladies of Isla Mujeres." As we walk along, attentive to our guide, Enrique takes my hand in his; so quietly and naturally.

Back on our scooters, Enrique takes the lead again. After about two miles, he turns off onto a private dirt road to a small beach of even finer glistening white sand. We lay out our towels on the beach and spend a few hours in the shade of a small palm tree. Plenty of silence and then some intimate private conversation about our lives and the impending journey to Havana.

"Enrique, you haven't told me what you do for a living or where you actually live," I say with curiosity.

"Ahh, si, I am an import/export entrepreneur. I get goods from one place in the world to another. I was able to get out of Cuba several years ago, because my uncle pretended that I was his son, and he was living in the U.S. on a medical education visa. It was a new life for me. Although I was already 30 years old then, he managed to get me to Miami. I was a lucky young man. My family is very tight. We take care of each other. Now I am legal in the U.S.A. I can also go back to Cuba to see relatives and visit my beloved culture; although again, I am not a big fan of the government. In truth, I hate Fidel Castro for good reason", Enrique confesses his strong feelings as he bangs his fist into the sand with serious force.

Wow, I think, Seeing his love and connection to his family and his passionate disapproval of Castro, I feel I am getting closer and closer to knowing this man.

His face close to mine, he speaks softly. "Let me be your escort and guide you tomorrow, so that you safely enter Cuba, without any hassles." He looks intently into my eyes with those large dark saucers.

"I wouldn't go any other way, Enrique. Of course, you know that I'm nervous about this journey."

"Sí, sí, but I will be there by your side. You will be in very good hands." He playfully shakes my hand. Keeping my hand in his and stroking it from time to time, we continue talking. We are intimate in our conversation, which goes on into the late afternoon.

I tell him more about what I do for a living, trying as best I can to describe the frenetic pace of my consulting work and my life in general. This includes humorous tales of my basset hound Clyde and a little about my best friend Carla. I don't mention Doug as my romantic significant other, only that I have a male business partner who actually lives in Seattle. When I excitedly talk about yesterday's parasailing adventure and how it has already overcome some of my mental fear of heights, he listens with great interest, happy for my accomplishment. He is intrigued also when I take the brilliant blue crystal wrapped in its royal blue cloth, from my backpack. I describe Gurjot, my encouraging Indian friend and his friendly family. Enrique gazes at the crystal in wonder. "It is a symbol of love and strength transferred to you from this Indian man," he philosophizes. "You know this, sí? It will help you be fierce when it is necessary. You never know when that might come in handy."

I nod; concurring. We lay there together on our stomachs, passing the crystal back and forth between us.

Back on the scooters, I follow Enrique through the curving turns and then up over some cliffs edging the coastline. The whole time I am saying, 'oh shit' in my mind. I wonder if Enrique is purposely pushing me to solidly prove that I am truly overcoming my fear of heights. I push forward with fortitude on my scooter, kicking my fear in the ass; matching his speed at every turn despite the sharp, edgy landscape - overcoming cliff after rocky cliff. He stops at a vista point. I look down – one of the steepest cliffs we've encountered on this ride. I feel intimidated but I overcome it in an instant. I become strong and confident. Pulling my camera from my backpack, I photograph the glorious vista, documenting my first experience standing on a steep cliff without being taken over by intense fear. Enrique smiles at me with pride. He jumps back on his scooter and again I'm right behind him. He leads, as we descend down the Isla Mujeres village road; then reduces his speed as we approach the center of town.

He stops at what looks like a beautiful Mexican villa. The sign outside reads: *LoLo Lorena.* "This is my favorite restaurant, Charlie. You will love this place. Lorena is another great head chef here in Mexico. She is the good friend of my cousin, Miguel.

I ask Enrique if there is a place where I change into my other clothes vs. wearing my jean shorts and bathing suit.

"Sí, sí, come with me."

He takes me around the corner to a public bathroom. I put on my purple cotton sun dress, matched with a light violet shawl and a pair of medium-heeled black patent leather sandals. As I exit the bathroom, my hair now up in a ponytail, I see that Enrique wears his black aloha shirt which is decorated with little green palm trees over a pair of nice light green Bermuda shorts. He sees me emerge and does a dramatic double-take.

"Nice tan, señora and the outfit - it is enchanting. You are a fairy tale princess."

He takes my hand, leading me back to LoLo Lorena's. The restaurant entrance opens into a beautiful garden lit by table-top candles. I have my camera in tow. The sun is down. The lights flicker and glow. The courtyard appears to seat maybe 15 guests for dinner; communal seating at three wooden tables – each decorated with colorful tablecloths and matching place-mats. The stars twinkle overhead. The uniquely designed garden court gets even more romantic by the minute. A lovely-looking hostess seats us, with nobody else sitting at our table for five. A bulky European-looking woman bolts out of the kitchen while I am busy photographing the flowers, plants and arrangement of tables which are topped with extravagantly patterned linens. I use my flash sparingly as the light is low; carefully ensuring I don't invade anyone's space.

The woman who just bolted from the kitchen, wears an embroidered apron. She spots Enrique and heads directly to our table. She has big deep blue eyes and chubby rosy cheeks. Lorena's accent is French. She jokes with Enrique about his cousin Miguel, sending her love back to him in Cancun.

I ask if I can photograph her so that Enrique may share it with Miguel. She's delighted. I photograph Lorena with Enrique. My ulterior motive is accomplished – a souvenir photo of Enrique. They stand close together, and then Lorena runs away to get a bouquet of flowers to hold while I take another shot of them. They start kidding around with various poses. Lorena puts some flowers in her bunned blonde hair; using a bobby pin which she pulls out from the back of her head. Both of them are having a great time mugging at the camera. I encourage them to pose in a variety of ways. I also catch plenty of candid shots between poses. Lorena gestures, inviting me to give her the camera. She signals that Enrique and I should have a photo together. She takes a large flower from another table and places it in my hair, using her bobby pin. Enrique pulls me to him, as we ready for the shot. He kisses me on the cheek and Lorena captures that one too. I am content and satisfied with this shot. We are now ready to eat!

As I examine the décor, including the gold-leafed wall fixtures, I feel like I've been transported to France; perhaps Aix en Provence. Lorena explains that she is actually from Belgium and that her special cuisine is indeed French, with a little Mexico thrown in, adding some special flavor blending. She adds, "Cette maison est trop jolie, n'est-ce pas?"

I reply, "Ah oui. J'aime toute les choses de Mexico et de France aussi." She is gleefully impressed.

"Vous parlez francais, mademoiselle?" she inquires.

I reply, "Oui, je parle francais un peu." We converse in French for another few minutes.

Enrique is stunned by this. "Dios mio. Dios mio. She speaks the French but not the more important Spanish language? Pour qué?" He says with a hint of sarcasm.

"Je ne sais pas," I respond back in my flawless French.

"You are still full of surprises Miss Charlotte Sweeney," he smiles.

Lorena gives us the run-down of her menu tonight; describing each dish with zest and passion. Famished, I go for the seafood cassoulet, topped with chorizo while Enrique waters his mouth and orders the seafood stew. What a combo we are! We share the thai prawn salad as an appetizer. Two of the largest light green margaritas arrive at our table, adorned with an array of fruit skewered by the longest toothpick I've ever seen. Enrique raises his glass to Lorena, who is now busy entertaining other guests; but she acknowledges his grand gesture with a smile. As we finish our entrees, the hostess surprisingly puts out the candles at each table. It is now pitch black in the courtyard.

Loud, drumming latin music plays, and two fire dancers appear right before our eyes. They toss sticks of fire into the air, and between each other - quickly and with adept skill. They dance with robust energy to the Mexican beat of the music. I am blown away by this, so close to our table. I can feel the heat on my face and arms. I am enchanted and almost mesmerized by this dramatic performance in such a small space. We finish our desert.

Before we leave, I notice several beautiful photographic portraits hung on the walls in the villa's foyer. I learn from Enrique that Lorena is also a well- known photographer; selling her work in Cancun and the surrounding area. Lorena kisses Enrique and hugs me as we depart, handing me a beautiful postcard souvenir, so that I won't forget LoLo Lorena's. We drive our scooters only a few blocks back to the ferry. It's about 9:30 pm and we are back at my hotel by 10:45.

At the hotel entrance, Enrique embraces me and gives me one little light kiss on the lips. "Buenas noches, Charlie. It has been a special day for me. I hope the same for you. Si? "

Taking initiative, I kiss him. "It was heaven for me. But I admit it; I am sleepy."

"I can see that. A long day. So - shall we meet here at 11 a.m.?" He is on the subject of tomorrow. The flight to Havana on Cubana Air that I recommend we catch, leaves at 1:20 pm."

I nod in agreement, rubbing my eyes. He hugs me one more time, kisses my forehead with his warm, soft lips, and then drives off in the vehicle adorned with the words: *Hacienda – A Restaurant For Love!*". I think to myself, Cancun – A Haven for Romance.

Chapter Eight

JOURNEY TO HAVANA

I sleep well. No dreams and gratefully, no bad flashbacks of Priscilla. I slept with my crystal under the pillow. Is it the crystal keeping my mind clear of the past tragedy or is it the new light of Enrique Ruiz in my life? Can either keep the haunting ghost of Priscilla away from my doorstep? I don't know.

Having packed my bags while half asleep last night, this morning I'm ready to grab breakfast and be outside the hotel lobby at 11 a.m. But before I leave my room, I take out Gurjot's sign from my backpack: *CHARLIE THE BRAVE ONE*! I stare at it, smiling – still feeling Gurjot's kindness once again, and place my hand over the letters slowly outlining them with my finger. In a very short time, Gurjot managed to cause significant personal change in my life; putting me on the road to overcoming my fear of heights. Now on the brink of going through this somewhat daunting entry into Cuba, I need to *be* the brave one. Mostly what I need is confidence Yes, lots of people have done this before me, and were careful. And I have a Cuban angel at my side to deal with the little challenges that crop up. Habana, Cuba – here I come! I have Gurjot's crystal. I can feel it will bring me luck. And maybe produce some magic!

Enrique stands outside the Royal Solaris lobby with his carry-on suitcase and satchel. I can see him from the hotel check-out area. I watch him from afar as I await my receipt from the desk clerk. Enrique stands in silence staring out beyond the hotel driveway, appearing deep in thought. A trio of pretty young women walk across the driveway and seem to be admiring this good-looking latin man; well-dressed and wearing his sporty dark sunglasses. Any woman would take a second or even third look in his direction. I can see the women give each other the eye, as if using a secret code for "wow, he's nice!" I get out there quickly to greet Enrique, catching one of the young girls turning around to stare in his direction for one last once over. He must be in high demand amongst the females in this town and others, I think.

Enrique gives me a gentle hug hello, and hails a taxi before the valet attendant has a chance to do the same. We are on our way. He pulls out some paperwork and explains that he's already purchased an airline ticket and just needs his boarding pass. In fact, he can go directly to the gate since he has only carry-on bags. I listen carefully to him.

"This is good," he explains. "It won't place us together in the eyes of the ticket agents or authorities; just to be extra safe." I have already checked on this. There are currently a number of available seats on this flight. You can easily purchase a ticket for the 1:00 p.m. flight. Just walk up to the Cubana Air counter, pay cash, and use a slip of white paper for stamping later vs. using your passport".

Enrique hands me a little pad of paper and a small pen. "Give this to the counter agent. You can request a seat in row 12. I think there is one still open right next to me or at least on the opposite aisle." He points to the assigned seat number on his ticket. I jot it down on the pad, so I won't forget.

At the ticket counter in the airport, my nerves are frayed. Enrique has proceeded through security to the gate. The airline counter staff member seems to understand my intent, as soon as I finish my first sentence. I hand him the cash in Mexican pesos. He hand me a boarding pass with a seat number but with no passenger name entered in the appropriate area. He does not seem to want to know my name. He gives me a bag-gage tag, also with no name indicated. Security is lax as I walk through. The man with the badge sitting on the stool checking boarding passes just peeks quickly at my passport, and does not even look at my boarding pass. It's as if there's an unspoken blind eye to Americans who want to enter Havana but who have no approved in advance visa. I get it. I guess they want visitors from everywhere. Cuba depends on tourism as well as the sale of cigars and other plantation goods. Anyway, it's the American side of customs and security that would have great concern for me entering Cuba; not so much the Cuban side, and probably not Mexico either. Remember, I silently remind myself – trad-ing with the enemy and all that. This concept seems archaic to me for a country like the U.S.

On the small commuter plane, I sit in the same row just across the narrow aisle from Enrique. He smiles at me and gives me a wink when I sit down. As we take to the air, with people all around us, and the two flight attendants already enraptured with his good looks and charm, Enrique introduces himself to me, as if we were total strangers on a plane; just meeting for the first time. He makes me laugh inside. I know that he is pur-posely being extra cautious. I appreciate his care and concern. And what is really great for me, is that I don't quiver in fear for the first time when going in for a landing. Enrique distracts me with his light and comedic conversation; keeping me laughing the whole time.

Once we touch down in Havana, with only a 45 minute flight behind us, he changes into an even more playful interaction style, starting with a tickle on my lower back as I struggle up the ramp into the arrival lounge, as I try to manage my array of usual carry-ons. My camera bag is now hanging down the front of my body from my neck. It's so heavy but I'm thoroughly enjoying Enrique's childlike spirit.

"Now, we are on my real turf – Cuba," he whispers in my ear from behind. "You must obey my every word when in my country, sí?" he teases as he takes the bags from me, a welcome repeat performance of our Cancun arrival just a few days ago. "I will get you to a good hotel. Let me recommend the most historic colonial Hotel Inglaterra in Old Habana. Okay for you?" he inquires.

"How can I say no when dealing with such a capable expert?" He sits close to me in the taxi, takes my hand and asks another question.

"By the way, do you speak any Spanish? I know that you, how you say, 'kick my Cuban ass' in the French department. I am just wondering. Is there another language surprise about you around the corner?"

"Well, I took Spanish for a few months once when I was teaching in the Bowery of New York, my first year out of college. All I can remember is, cuántos diás hayen en la semana?"

He bursts out laughing in disbelief. "How many days are there in the week?" He translates my awkward pronunciation into English. "You kid me. Right Charlie? Why would you remember only that sentence?" He bursts out laughing; enjoying my ridiculous memory of a useless Spanish phrase.

I assure him that I have no idea why I chose this sentence to remember. Perhaps it was the first thing I ever learned in Spanish and from then on I was zoned out. Anyway, I can probably figure out some Spanish words as many of them have a similar derivation as French words – both romance languages with Latin as the foundational source.

"Ah, sí." He says this in jest, not really knowing what I'm talking about here.

We are now entering the inner city – Old Havana. It's a photographer's Disneyland; nirvana for me – like a drug I am unable to resist. I can't wait to get out there and click away. The old cars, the architecture, the colors. Yes, a lot of run down stuff everywhere, street after busy street. It's like I've been thrown back into the 1950's. I can't take my eyes off the people. They are more than interesting. Many look hot and weathered but as a people, they seem to have a dignity about them, contrasted by their sultry body movements. The adults ooze sensuality as they walk down the streets. The children are intense - running and yelling to their friends. I roll the window down and start shooting – click, click, click. Every moment, another shot I must capture.

Enrique smiles, understanding and quietly supporting my eagerness.

"Enrique, the pastel colors are beautiful," I sing out.

"Hmm-mmm - Si,"he agrees, observing me. "I am in total agreement. Incredible colors… the blue eyes, golden hair, light brown skin. I am loving the colors of you!"

My heart is pounding," he says as he looks me up and down.

I laugh and give him a playful jab in the arm, enjoying his ogling me with his eyes, as well as his flattering remarks. We turn into a large intersection, now riding down a wide and bustling avenue.

"That is the Hotel Nacional," he offers, "an old and very elegant hotel. In fact, it used to be the center of the Cuban government, but is now an expensive tourist-only hotel. I am personally not a big fan of this place, but indeed, the architecture inside and outside is breathtaking." Then we pass the Museum of The Revolution. I don't ask Enrique anything on this. Seems like a sore subject.

As we approach our destination, I see the hotel sign sculpted in stone at the top of the hotel as well as a more modern electric blue sign running down the side corner of the classic building. Several tall palm trees surround a street side parking lot which is full of 1950's Ford Fairlanes and other dated cars from 50-60 years ago. Old iron street lamps are scattered between the palms, and rows of hotel room terraces look out onto the scene. The hotel is only four stories high, white stone colonial style architecture, as Enrique had described. I see a very old theatre across the street, another incredible design accomplishment, with impressively crafted detail everywhere the eye can see.

Another old building shares a wall on the other side of The Hotel Inglaterra, boasting similar colonial architecture. Crumbling pastel buildings all around us mixed in with the greatly preserved, cared for structures. The street sign reads Habana Viejo. I vow to myself to shoot these streets from dawn till dusk, and into the evening the next day. Our taxi comes to a stop at the hotel entrance.

"And now, you will experience one of the finest Habana hotels, built in - believe it or not, the year 1875." Enrique seems excited for me. " I will secure you the best room facing the Parque Central, complete with a splendid balcony for your photographic pleasure. This room is number 324. I hope it is still available," he says before we leave the taxi. He invites me to exit the car as he comes around to open my door, with a slight bow a la Prince Charming. While Enrique pays the driver, I see the inviting outdoor bar where couples sit and chat over late afternoon cocktails and coffees. I also notice a heavily painted prostitute being literally pushed away by the hotel doorman. Once he manages to re-locate her a fair distance from the front entrance, he starts cajoling with her; openly flirting. What a conundrum; two opposite behaviors from one person in a split second. A group of European looking tourists rush out of the hotel, joking loudly in German. I see one of them flag down a young boy, purchasing some cigars. Cuban music comes from the outdoor bar. A lot of activity is going on. It's overwhelming, yet so much fun.

My eyes are immediately drawn to the ornate gold and white carved high ceilings inside the hotel. The lobby is not huge but quaint, with plenty of character. Hanging above the reception desk is a beautiful royal blue stained glass window, finished with gold leaf which looks art deco in style. Enrique goes quickly to the counter as I stroll around, delighted with his choice of hotel. I am more than pleased to be staying at such a treasured Old Havana landmark and feel lucky to have met this handsome, kind Cuban man.

He appears to know the hotel reception clerk quite well. As Enrique returns to me, I notice a definite spring in his step. "You are one lucky American, Charlie Sweeney. Room 324 is available.

Now booked for 7 nights. You can make it more or less time, as you wish. This room is very special and full of beautiful Cuban antiquities; as I say before, with a perfect view of the park and city. You can pay at the end of your stay. They are trusting and know that you will pay cash, sí?"

I am so impressed listening to him. He's really taking care of me. "But you will need to wait about twenty minutes for the room to be ready. You can sit on the big sofa over there. If you say yes, I will go back to reception and do the final secure of this room for you." "That sounds good," I say this somewhat hesitantly thinking he may have the wrong impression. I am getting a little worried. He catches onto my suddenly concerned facial expression. My cheeks are turning red again; I am sure.

"No…no…señora Charlie. Please – please don't worry. I have no intention of sharing your room with you. I am visiting with my mother for this week; although I want to spend as much time as possible with you – if you will allow it. I want simply for you to enjoy the best in Old Habana. This hotel is very special."

"Oh," I say embarrassed by my personal leap, jumping to the conclusion that Enrique has a secret sexual, salacious scenario in mind for us.

"You know, I got you a very good discount on the room," he kids me to lighten things up. Then he gets serious, "Would you like to be alone tonight then or would a drink at the hotel café and then enjoying some authentic Cuban food be acceptable? Of course, escorted by your new Cuban friend, Enrique Ruiz. " He bows again - just slightly this time.

I look him up and down, considering how to respond; mocking him a bit. "I would love your company Enrique, but shouldn't you spend your first night home with your mother? "Wouldn't she expect that?" I ask sincerely.

He grins at me. "Charlie, you are right. How about if I spend a few hours with mi madre, and then meet you in the outdoor cafe bar at 8:00 p.m.? This is the best spot in town for observing the culture of Habana. "

I am so happy that Enrique wants more time with me, and so soon. "Yes, yes, of course. Once a Cuban hero, always a Cuban hero – sí? You are indeed my Dudley Do Right."

He looks at me quizzically, much like the last time I mentioned this cartoon character. I wave my hand with a 'never mind' gesture. I deliberately and flirtatiously flash my blue eyes at him. Okay – I'm working it now, trying to recover from my inaccurate and sinister sexually-based assumption about this wonderful man. I don't want him to think I distrust him. Geez, what is wrong with me? He has done nothing to make me question his sincerity. And truth be told, I probably trust this man more than dozens I've met throughout my life and more than many I've known for a long time. "

"But there is one thing, Enrique, I'd like us to agree. Tonight the dinner and drinks will be my treat."

His face and body cringe at my words. "No, no - it is not possible. We are Latin, si? In my country, a man wines and dines the woman – not the other way around. He looks at me sternly. I acquiesce with a nod and an understanding smile. I guess I can live with that." I don't want to break the Cuban macho spell. I like it.

"Bien. Bien," he says. "I will go back to reception to secure the room for you." While he does this, I walk over to the large red velvet lobby sofa and dump my things down beside me.

As I open my backpack to check on my Nikon paraphernalia, I hear a young boy's voice close by. I look up.

"Hola, lady...you want to buy Cuban cigars?" He looks to be about 11 years old. He's wears a mismatched patterned plaid tee shirt and grubby print pants. One of his sneaker laces is untied.

"Oh, hola to you. Well...I don't really smoke," I say. The boy looks dejected and starts to walk away. "But," I yell out, "Back home, I do have a boyfriend Doug who might really enjoy some Cuban cigars straight from Havana. How much are they?" I ask this question just as Enrique returns from the reception desk.

Damn, I can tell that Enrique has overheard my last two sentences. Now standing at the sofa, he says, "Señora, you have just, how you say, 'burst my bubble. Forgive me, I am still learning anglo expressions."

I laugh nervously and glance at the boy who smiles back thoroughly enjoying the adult dialogue. "Yes Enrique," we do say, 'burst my bubble' in the states. It is a common American idiom. But what do you mean by this?"

"Ahh, I only hope that in spite of your boyfriend back home that your heart is still open to meeting new special friends...like me. I can see that you are no longer in the closet with me about this man Doug."

"In the closet?" I question him for clarity. "Whoa, you definitely need to keep studying those American idioms."

Nodding, he pulls me up from the sofa, and peers deep into my eyes. "Perhaps you will have time to give me some private English language lessons here in Habana," he says, as he playfully covers the boy's ears. The boy laughs heartily, almost dropping some of his cigars from the carrying case hanging from his neck.

"Have you already found a new Cuban man to replace me?" He laughs and shakes Juan's hand. "Hola, hombre," Enrique greets him. As he starts to leave, Enrique shouts, "Hasta luego then Charlie. See you tonight at 8:00 o'clock in the café bar. Reception will bring your key over to the sofa in a few minutes. Adíos," he waves goodbye to the boy. We both wave back.

"Lady, I think that Cuban man really like you," the boy kids me. "Be careful. You be very careful with that man. Okay?"

I'm somewhat surprised by this child's warning. "So, you want this box of cigars for ten dollar?" He waves a single cigar in my face. "Good stuff, smell this one. It's the Gran Corona - nine inches long. A box of these are fifteen dollar. They come straight from the factory in Pinar del Río."

"Wow," I approve," after a quick whiff. "I will take the box for fifteen dollars. Si."

He is duly excited and gets one of the boxes ready for me from his pack. "By the way, what is your name?" I ask.

He stands up straight, as tall as can be. "I am Juan José Duarte. Ten years old and very smart. I am your new friend, si?"

Juan José Duarte is definitely a schmoozer, playing his clientele like an instrument, and putting me instantly at ease. " I know the English better than that man who just left," Juan José boasts. His dimples deepen as he flashes a broad smile. "I study for many years lady. If I don't know a lot of English, I cannot work the turistas and sell the most cigars. English is the most common language even with those turistas from Germany or Holland. They don't understand a lot of Spanish, you know lady?"

"Sí, sí," I nod. The man from the reception desk approaches me. "Señora, your room is ready. Here is your key. The room number is inscribed right there on the key. You pay cash when you leave. Your friend, Enrique has arranged this."

I smile in appreciation, taking the antique, heavy key. The elegantly uniformed man stares down at Juan José. He is dripping with disdain for this boy, and shoots him a disgusted glance. I can see that he's assumed the boy is doing nothing but hounding me.

I notice Juan José's untied sneaker. He's wearing Converse high tops. For goodness sakes. I love Cons; they remind me of New York City, my hometown. This boy is actually very cool; sporting the deepest dimple dents I've ever seen and a great head of dark shiny black hair; a contrast his soiled clothing. Except for those cool shoes! The man from reception leaves us, with a shooing away motion to Juan Jose, who temporarily backs off and then quickly returns to me, once the man is far enough away.

"That guy is out to get me," he grumbles. He knows I sell cigars. The hotel wants me to do this. But he acts like I'm a criminal everyday. Hey, you think you might want more cigars tomorrow?"

I feel sympathy for Juan José. He removes an object from his pocket. It looks like an old scratched watch face but without an accompanying wristband. He quickly looks at it and says,

"Oh lady, I need to go. Got to meet my sister Marta down at the Malécon. See you." He turns to go.

"Sure, probably see you tomorrow. Nice to meet you." He shouts out as he walks away, "Hey lady, what's your name? You no tell me."

"It's Charlie." I yell back to him, as he walks away".

He stops and laughs. "Charlie, hey that's a boy's name. You are one funny lady." Still chuckling to himself, he shakes his head, and rushes away.

Entering my room at The Hotel Inglaterra, I'm delighted at the authentic antiquity of the furniture. Although fairly simple décor, every piece is unique; and very old. The TV is equipped with worn dog ears; straight out of the 1950's. I open the drapes and step out onto the small balcony, feeling the history of all those who've stayed here before me. The street scene grabs me. My poor Nikon will poop out from exhaustion here in Havana. "It's okay baby." I pat my camera, with love.

As I look out on this neighborhood, I see a city of contrasts and contradictions. Poverty and wealth side by side; both extremes situated within the same square block. Each tourist attraction appears immaculate; hotels, theatres, and some restaurants. I also notice the run down tenements across the way. A dark-skinned man drops a bucket attached to a ragged rope from a third floor window. He is standing up, and I can see that he's practically naked except for his tattered underwear. He has a long scraggly gray beard, a bony body; and a cigarette dangling from his mouth. He lowers a rusty metal bucket to a young man down below on the street. The man dumps a sack of something into the bucket. Looks like grains of some sort. They yell back and forth as the old man pulls up the bucket, bumping it into other windows as he tries to maneuver the booty up to his level. The old man is frail and yet strong at the same time. I have a party with my Nikon as I click away; shot after candid shot – like a skilled voyeur. Close-ups of the old man's face are my trophies.

Looking down the street the other way, I can see the La Floridita bar sign. Now, that place is famous; an old hangout of Ernest Hemingway, who lived in and loved Havana. I remember reading that their daiquiris are 'to die for,' - a daily tribute to Hemingway. I must have one of their signature drinks in the next day or so. I zoom in for the shot of the sign jutting out from La Floridita's entrance, just as the streetlights turn on throughout Old Havana.

The sun is down and a new set of people are quickly appearing in this busy neighborhood. I adjust my exposure controls, grab my favorite filter - perfect for dusk photography, and shoot the architecture (doors, windows and balconies), as well as capture a flurry of people shots. I sing out, "Welcome to The Hotel Inglaterra," dancing across my room - while slowly unpacking. "Welcome to the Hotel Inglaterra, Such a lovely place. Such a lovely place." I take out the blue crystal gifted by Gurjot and my small framed photograph of Priscilla, me and my brother Sam. The three of us are giving each other a high five, as we smile for the camera. I place the photo on the side table by the antique iron bed and the crystal under my pillow.

Chapter Nine

HAVANA — A DATE TO REMEMBER

At 7:45 pm, I am dressed - clean hair and clean clothes. My royal blue and black flowered silk halter dress is a bit wrinkled but fits nicely, showing off my tan. My hair hangs loosely down my back, and is full with wavy volume from the Cuban humidity. I attach a small white flowered hair pin to the right side – just for a touch of sultriness. Anything I can muster is good. I know I don't look close to sexy compared to the natural sensuality of the typical Cuban female. Maybe a dab of Tresor, by Lancome, will help me. I spray my neck and wrists lightly.

The phone jingles. "I'm sipping a mojito here in the café; and I have one waiting for you. The people watching is 'from the gods'. You will love it Charlie." His voice. I heat up. I was needing my Enrique fix. Seems like I long to hear his voice at least once every three hours.

"I'll be down in one moment." Gathering my purse and my camera, I imagine Enrique kissing me. Maybe that will happen tonight. Shit, I forgot to try to phone Doug last night before leaving Cancun. Quickly, my mind flashes again to Enrique. Yes, I look forward to him kissing me. He hasn't been at all lecherous; but I can see in his eyes and through his remarks, that he is smitten. At least, I think so. My blood is running faster and hotter here in Havana. I feel it rushing through my veins at mach speed. I admit to myself that I'm open to anything.

Enrique sits at the table on the edge of the café, with a great view of the foot traffic in and out of the hotel. Cuban music plays in the background. The café is crowded. Enrique holds up his cocktail in greeting as I arrive. "I am looking at an exceptional vision of loveliness." He politely stands and toasts me. "Charlie, I would like to introduce you to your new Cuban friend – the mojito…a delicious rum cocktail adored by both the local people and even by the likes of Signor Ernest Hemingway." I take a sip and make my new acquaintance.

"Delicious! Is that a giant mint leaf in my glass?" I ask.

"Sí, refreshing, isn't it?"

I take another big sip. People are everywhere. Prostitutes are hustling tourists at a table closest to the street. Juan José, the boy I met earlier, is near by selling cigars to some Europeans. A peddler is offering jewelry, showing off his wares to tourists as they walk by. A trio of tall well-dressed, sexy Cuban woman emerge from a taxi; appearing ready for some dining and dancing. The place is humming. The head waiter is now scolding the prostitute to move away. A love-hate relationship going on there, I think, The rich, seductive and sultry culture surrounds me in this cafe.

"A great choice for my first night in Havana, Enrique."

He smiles. "You are a passionate woman, I can see that Charlie.

I try to respond and I'm apparently having a rough time. What the hell is happening? I can't seem to get the words out." I – I feel…. My eyes fail to focus for some reason. Am I just sleepy, overwhelmed by the humidity? The image of Enrique across from me seems to go in and out of my consciousness. My eyes, now blurred, wander over to the Hotel Inglaterra's front entrance. I'm fading…almost catatonic, in some kind of stupor. A small skinny man wearing a fedora hat and white pants leans against the building, and seems to be staring at me. He looks familiar. Why? I can see his black ponytail hanging down his back. Wait a minute…. He gets blurry too. I think he's dangling a key chain from his hand, twirling it around and around. Is he hypnotizing me? I'm so sleepy. Shit, I can't…

My head is thumping. I can't move. My body feels like lead. Sweat rolls down my temples, then sideways into my hair. It's hot, too hot. I can't breathe. My eyes struggle to open. A dangling light bulb hangs above me from a rusty linked chain. The light in the room is dim. I see the window shades are drawn. My headache worsens as I become a bit more conscious. My lips are sticky. I manage to turn my face sideways, the drool escaping from my mouth, as I scan for a clue to tell me where I am. I attempt to understand what is happening to me. An old woman sits on a dingy chair in the corner. She is holding an object, something on her lap. I don't know what it is. I ache, but persevere to turn my head to the other side, realizing that I am lying on a small cot in the middle of a smelly, almost bare room. That man, that small man with the fedora is standing by the shade-covered window. He looks bored. Shit, it's the same man from the Hotel. Fuck, it's the man from Cancun – the waiter; the one that I thought Enrique was talking to on the beach. I'm sure that's him. I notice the long dark ponytail again. Geez, I'm so groggy. My vision - still going in and out, focused and then unfocused. then focused again. Is this another one of my bad dreams?

A larger man walks over to the small man who wears the fedora. Oh god, it's Enrique. Shit! Shit, has he abducted me? What the hell, I think; now panicking but afraid to move and alert my captors. It's as if the earth's gravitational pull has grasped my heartstrings, yanking them tighter and tighter; squeezing them with the most brutal force. This man has betrayed me, I realize it now. Fucking Enrique! My heart has been cracked open like some fragile egg, smashed up against a wall and now lies splattered in a messy puddle on the dirty floor. I am broken. Lost, scared, fallen, vulnerable; but fucking angry.

I attempt to get up from the sagging mattress and run. Escape! I almost fall to the floor, my body too heavy to lift itself from the cot. Enrique rushes over to me, tries to take hold of me. I beat him with my fists, pound him in his face, on his head. I'm not having any impact. I am too weak. I try to kick him with all my might; but I am still too weak to have an effect. My legs feel like rubber. Shit, he drugged me. This notion hits me with hurricane force. I ache everywhere - in my body and in my soul.

"You drugged me! You drugged me! I attempt to yell at him, my voice weak and scratchy.

"Charlie, Charlie, calm down," he says. Please, please, it's okay. You are fine," he begs me to listen. "I'm so happy you're awake."

Trying to get up again, I just fall back down like a sack of potatoes – empty of any strength. I want to throw things at him. I want to kill him. My fight, flight response is now in full force. Nothing he can say will stop me from going. He'll have to kill me. I throw the blanket off my body which covers me. "Why did they cover me with a blanket when it's so fucking hot in here?"

Helpless, I lay back down and become quiet again. The little energy I mustered is now drained from my body. If I'm drugged, just forget it Charlie, I think to myself. Is he going to rape me? Is he going to kill me? Who are these people – that man with the hat, that old woman? My mind races in every direction. Enrique looks down at me. I hear a baby cry out. I must be hallucinating. Shit, who the hell are these people?

"Charlie, please listen." he whispers now. The baby is now whimpering, no longer crying.

"Fuck you," I say to Enrique. "You liar, you fooled me. You're committing a serious crime you moron. Did you or did you not drug me? Bastard!"

His head hangs, and this time, it's his sweat that drips onto me. Not some fake tears like in Cancun. Everything he did, every-thing he said has been a fucking lie. A fraud!

"Yes," he says solemnly. "I drugged you. I needed to get you to this place, where nobody would know what we are up to. I did fuck up. I don't know why I went to this length. Miguel advised me to do this instead of just talking...."

"Fuck you, I break in, the tears and rage now flowing full blast from my slowly recovering body. I manage to sit up. Did he say Miguel, his cousin was in on this? The small man with the fedora speaks in Spanish to Enrique. He sounds worried and looks nervous. He is complaining.

"Carlos, no lo hagas. No lo hagas! Cállate!" Enrique ignores him.

"I fucking hate you Enrique!" I am able to scream more loudly now and smack him with more force square in his face. The baby cries out.

"What the hell is going on here? Tell me." I yell this even more loudly. Maybe someone will hear me. "This baby, this woman, that man. He's the one from Cancun, right?" I want him to feel my anger – my hate for him. "What do you want? WHY?"

"It's a big mistake, Charlie. I know this looks very bad. I slipped a small sedative in your mojito.

"Fuck you. There is no such thing as a small sedative, you asshole!" I respond with heightened anger.

The baby is crying again. The old woman speaks to Enrique in Spanish. He responds,

"Sí Mama. Si Doña Lia. Comprendes," he nods to her in understanding. Still sitting on my cot, he speaks softly. "Charlie, the baby is scared. I understand that you are mad at me. Honestly, my family just needs your help."

I can't believe my ears. My head is still pounding from the sedative. "My help? Then why drug me? Why this cloak and dagger routine?"

Enrique nods, "I understand how you feel," he says. "But pardon - what is cluck and dagger?" I'm not laughing this time at his inept comprehension of American idioms.

"Never mind...forget about cloak and dagger. You kidnapped me, you comprendes that?" I snap.

Enrique gets up and paces the floor in silence. "Hear me out Charlie. Just for a few minutes. Listen to my pathetic story. Just give me five minutes more, You are only ten steps away from The Hotel Inglaterra. I promise you. I will take you back there immediately after I explain this scene. Trust me!" He pleads again.

"Trust you? Why should I? When you've lied to me; abducted me? You and your crazy compadres. Okay fine, explain yourself, go ahead!"

He sits down on the edge of my cot, at the far end. "I have a sister Marguerita. She and her husband Ferdinand were both active supporters of Cubans Against Castro policies. Both young surgeons at Habana's Children's Hospital. Six months ago, Marguerita and Ferdinand escaped Cuba after leading a public protest against food shortages and the unjust incarceration of many Cubans who have committed nothing but peaceful activities. Si, peaceful things like writing letters of complaint to the government or demonstrations outside government buildings".

I listen, but I grow impatient with his explanation. "Get to the point," I demand. "I see you are concerned about your family, but what does this have to do with drugging me?"

I manage to get up from the bed. I glance over at his elderly mother and the baby she is holding in her arms. I notice that this baby has blonde curly hair. She now sleeps in a baby chair on the floor by the old woman.

"Whose baby is this Enrique? Is this baby girl yours?" He moves close to me.

"No, this is what I was trying to explain but not very well. The baby's name is Theresa and she belongs to Marguerita and Ferdinand. Theresa is my niece."

"Your niece! And I was kidnapped because…?" He walks over to his mother whom he referred to as Doña Lia.

"Because…" He pauses and I see he's choking up. "Because we want you to smuggle little Theresa to Miami – and pretend to be her mother."

I can't believe what I'm hearing. My anger rushes back to me. "He's an idiot," I think. I don't want to continue yelling and wake the sleeping baby. I speak in low tones but still with anger and disbelief. "You want me to pretend to be this baby's mother and commit a completely criminal act on top of me already entering Cuba illegally? Are you crazy? Are you insane?"

"Wait, there is more to the story," he continues.

"I don't care." I think about it for a moment. "Okay, then. Go on!" I reluctantly agree to hear more.

"Gracias Charlie. While Marguerita and Ferdinand were leading a peaceful Habana protest, a Cuban army guard was accidentally killed…impaled by a wooden stake which held a pro-test sign. It was a surging crowd of passionate protesters."

"God, am I hearing a banter of more lies here?"

"Nothing…nothing to do with my sister or with her husband. It was just an accident. A tragedy." Enrique sits down on the small cot. He pauses, shaken.

"Just another ruse," I think. "That's all!" I pledge to myself not to succumb to feeling any sympathy for this abominable man. Never! "Geez Enrique. Are you just giving me more crap here? More lies?"

The baby squirms in her chair. Doña Lia rises to pick her up, comforting and caressing her with her thin, wrinkled arms.

"May I finish this ugly story?" Enrique asks.

I nod in silence.

"Castro took advantage of this accident."

"*The Fidel Castro*?" I inquire sarcastically.

"Yes, Castro knew about the activities of Marguerita and Ferdinand. He put a $10,000 reward on their heads. Cajaron! Son of a bitch! He wanted them – either dead or alive. His wish was to use them as an example. Of course, we're all human. Cuban families would do anything for money…especially this much money."

I weaken a little. "Oh my god. Are they in jail then? They're not dead? This little baby is not an orphan?"

He shakes his head. "No…no…thank god. We managed to get the two of them out of Cuba within 24 hours of the announcement from Castro. We did this through family friends…civil rights supporters. Marguerita and Ferdinand are in Miami now…working in a hospital with false papers."

Doña Lia feeds a bottle of milk to Theresa. I can hear the baby girl sucking furiously.

"So, how exactly did they escape?" Now – I'm curious.

"We have a Cuban friend who managed to arrange this. Disguises. False passports. Not easy Charlie. But they made it out; escaped the wrath of Castro."

"So why didn't they take the baby with them?" I ask; still not trusting him an inch.

"Little Theresa was only four months old and sick with a spinal virus. Very dangerous. We didn't want to risk it."

"This baby, this Theresa," I say as I move towards Doña Lia. "She is blonde and blue eyed. Come on Enrique, how can she be Cuban? How? It's a joke!" I look into the baby's blue eyes now. However, I do notice how her skin is dark brown.

"Sí, and this is why we chose you Charlie."

"Chose me? Chose me?" I sarcastically laugh.

Enrique picks up the baby and comes to me. "Ferdinand's grandmother was born in Norway. She married a Cuban construction worker – Juan Carlo. The whole family was as surprised as you to see this baby's golden hair and her sea blue eyes. I tell you the truth here, Charlie."

I think for a minute. "I guess she could be taken as my daughter, but there is no way I would ever do this insane thing. It's like suicide." Yes, as transparent a suicide as Priscilla's, I think as I gaze again into Theresa's speckled blue eyes. She touches my nose with her tiny hand, making baby sounds. She points to my freckles.

I look up at Enrique as he cuddles Theresa. "So you picked me because I fit the profile – blonde hair, blue eyes, and as dumb as a doorknob, right?"

Enrique appears confused by my last statement.

"Never mind! Never mind!" I'm annoyed. He doesn't understand 'as dumb as a doorknob,' I guess.

"It's another idiom Enrique. Why kidnap me? Why not just ask me like a civilized person? This barbaric fiasco... this charade of being my new Cuban friend...your silly romantic front..."

He goes to touch my hair. I swat his hand away. "It was stupido," he admits. "We were desperate. I...I don't know. I thought if we took you to an unknown place, then asked you to do this risky thing. I thought if you saw Theresa in this private place. You don't understand..."

"Yes, I do understand. I am just a pawn for you. A pathetic dope. An American nitwit."

"No, you don't understand everything yet. You see, there is one more thing. Marguerita has been diagnosed with breast cancer...just a month ago."

Absorbing yet more new information, I fall back down onto the cot and lay there like a mummified corpse. Then – I sit up and hold my head in my hands, exasperated. My brain is exploding. My emotions have been sucked dry. Why does he do this to me? It just gets worse and worse by the second.

Enrique continues. "Marguerita wants to see her baby. Theresa can also be re-united with her father. My hope is that Marguerita will survive her cancer; especially when she has the motivation to live right in front of her – her beautiful baby."

Doña Lia takes Theresa from Enrique. She strokes her blonde curly hair. "Mi nina dulce. Mi niña dulce," she tenderly comforts the baby.

"It is a stupido plan, I admit." Enrique smacks himself on the head.

"Yes," I say, "it is stupid, and very risky – putting me in dire straights, and don't ask me what that means! I can't take this baby anywhere. We'll get caught and I'll wind up in prison!" Then it hits me. It hits me like a bomb exploding right between my eyes. The whole frigging thing was planned from the beginning.

Me, bumping into him at SFO. Me, spending time with him in Cancun. Him, knowing that I had intended to enter Havana through Mexico.

Enrique looks exhausted. He should be. Who cares? I think to myself.

"I will take you back to your room now," he says. As I said, you are really only ten steps away from your hotel. This is an abandoned loft we are in now." He approaches me, handing me my purse. "Lo siento. Forgive me Charlie. I've made a bad mistake and I am sorry from deep inside my heart."

"Just one more thing," I say. "How did I become your chosen one?" He moves away. Obviously, he doesn't want to look at me, doesn't want to face me. He takes the baby again from Doña Lia.

"Please don't be upset Charlie, but I have been in touch with a close friend of yours."

"Close friend?" I question him.

"Sí…she knows about this…how you say…our plot to smuggle little Theresa out of Cuba. Carla – your friend Carla – she is actually a relative of mine."

I am numb. His last words start to penetrate, etch themselves into my mind. I didn't think it could get worse than fifteen minutes ago. Betrayal – a no-nonsense dose of reality! Another hand grenade thrown down in my path. Another tidbit of shrapnel now embedded under my skin.

"She's my friend, why didn't she just ask me herself?" I scream at him.

"Listen, please. Carla did not know that I would kidnap you, or take you here. The plan was just to have us meet by accident, come to Havana together, and then I would ask you to do the smuggling."

Enrique approaches again, then reaches out to touch me. I yank myself away, even though he's got the baby in his arms.

"Miguel urged me to abduct you. Not Carla."

"Charlatans, all of them," I think to myself. "Leave me alone. Don't put a finger on me ever again. You understand? I don't want you to escort me anywhere. Have that man – that man with his ridiculous looking hat, guide me out of this building. I can find my own way after that!"

"Si, he is my cousin Carlo. He will take you downstairs."

"Geez, is everyone his freaking cousin?"

Enrique speaks to Carlo with a harried hushed tone. I assume he's requesting him to escort me safely out of the building; and then let me go. I grab my purse from the cot. I think I can walk now without feeling the heavy weight of the sedative in spite of my emotional breakdown. I slam the door behind me. We descend a dusty, dimly lit staircase and arrive at the rusty door, the welcome exit from the building.

It's dark outside; must be past midnight – maybe one a.m. The humidity seems even greater than in the heat of the afternoon sun. The street is still crowded with people enjoying a night out - celebrating their weekend; as if nothing evil has happened in this town tonight. But I know better. Cuban beats spill out from every restaurant, every bar. The music is no longer pleasant, no longer enticing – just unwanted noise to me now!!! My head throbs. My mind is reeling. My anger - ebbing and flowing, as I walk aimlessly, passing right by my hotel entrance. What am I doing? My haze continues. I turn back, plugging along step by step.

My mind travels to the concept of true friendship which will never mean much to me again. My best friend Carla has betrayed me day after day. For how long? Who cares if she didn't know about the abduction. She still lied to me; set me up to meet and fall for Enrique. All I want is to go home – escape this hell, hug my dog Clyde and my brother Sam. Never take them for granted again.

Chapter Ten

REALITY — IT'S A BITCH!

can barely turn the metal key to open my hotel room door.
Once I enter the suite, falling onto the once admired antique
brass bed, I fall again, only this time into uncontrollable tears.
I weep until I transition into a restless sleep, still in my clothes,
hunched up like a fetus, wishing I was never born. I yearn for my
sister, someone to truly understand the torture of my breaking
heart. I was almost in love with that man. I also no longer have a
best friend; and sadly I never did. Carla was merely a mirage, an
apparition, probably fooling me for several years; meticulously
leading me smack into the hands of yet another liar. I whisper
into my soaking wet pillow, "Priscilla, why did you leave me? I
need you – my only true female friend."

Two dismal dreams are in store for me tonight. My hiatus
from the bad 'Priscilla' dreams has ended. Dark scenes are back
with a vengeance; ready to haunt me when I need rest. Taunting
me when I need serenity more than ever . The first dream I have
tonight is my visualization of what probably happened the day
Priscilla ended her life. Only a few hours before she inhaled
those deadly car fumes in her garage, only a few hours before
her young son finds her dead at the wheel of her Toyota hatchback, she finalizes her exit plan. She'd been thinking about it
for weeks but that day it became crystal clear what she must do.
While her two boys are at school, her baby girl is in daycare, her

husband muddles along at his workplace and with herself free, free as a bird, Priscilla takes total control of the last few hours of life. I see her in those final moments – not crying, no longer in pain, her decision made, the ambiguity of her life now resolved. She prepares the house; vacuums every room twice, scrubs the bathtub and toilets until spic and span, and even cooks 7 days of meals in advance, popping the various entrees into freezer bags.

Priscilla feels confident that she has taken care of her family for at least seven days past her planned departure from the living. I see Pris' face just before her hand touches the kitchen door which opens into the garage, which leads to the Toyota – to the two ton metal murder weapon. In my dream, she takes a final moment before stepping down into the garage to make sure she has turned off the oven after her morning baking spree. She washes her hands at the kitchen sink and wipes them dry on the tea towel hanging from the fridge magnet, where a photo of her two boys smile back at her one last time. She descends that short staircase into her garage, later known as the crime scene.

Her suicide cave is waiting. She removes the gas tank cap and stuffs the hole with a thick blue towel, ensuring her plan will have a successful outcome; a peaceful death – like falling asleep. Pris knows that no family member will be home for at least two more hours. She is sitting in her car, her head limp, then hitting the steering wheel; her last breathe escaping onto the black dashboard. "Stop Priscilla, open the door", I plead into my pillow.

I awake with a start to the loud sound of the Havana hotel room ceiling fan. Whoosh after whoosh, after irritating whoosh. No air conditioning in this old hotel, only fans to fool you into believing you are cooler than the 90 degree temperature, than the 98 per cent humidity. At least Carla was right about the Cuban humidity. Everything else she ever said to me was a freaking lie! I grab my watch which lights up in the dark. It's four a.m. Wet with sweat, I'm still feeling the effects of the damn sedative. Sick to my stomach, I rush to the bathroom. I throw up in the toilet and drag my body back to the bed. Still exhausted, I drift off into sleep once again.

My second dream re-plays an actual scene from about 18 months ago, only nine months after the birth of Priscilla's third child. I'm visiting her in Florida, spending two nights with Pris and her family before I attend an Orlando Human Resources conference. A lucky break for me, a business event in Florida where I can also visit my sister and meet her latest family addition. In this dream, we all sit at their dinner table – me, Pris, her husband Jack, her two young boys and the baby girl in her high chair.

Jack barks an order to Pris, "More meat, more ribs!" He looks dirty, his tee shirt shredded around the collar and his hands dripping with barbecue sauce as he rips the last chunk of meat from the bone. "More meat – didn't ya hear me?" he shouts louder, banging his fist on the shabby table. The boys and Priscilla all cringe. I can see they live in fear of Jack; and it's not just based on tonight's sideshow.

"Yes, Jack, I'll get it," Pris skittishly replies. "Take it easy," she adds, embarrassed in front of me – the family relation who only visits once every couple of years.

Pris rushes to the kitchen. The baby starts to fuss once she notices her mommy has disappeared from the room. Pris returns with a hot plate full of sizzling ribs. The baby girl's whimpers have now turned into a full blown screaming session. Pris is frazzled and torn, dropping a couple of ribs onto the floor as she tries to transfer them to Jack's dinner plate with her metal tongs.

"Shit! God damn – what the hell's wrong with you?" He raps the table again but this time with heightened anger and increased force. He doesn't help her with the mess nor does he consider attending to his crying baby. Pris wipes her apron and picks up the two fallen ribs, her hands now smothered in barbecue sauce. She attempts to clean up the mess. Jack grabs her skirt as she's bending down – her feet slipping on the floor. "Gimme that fucking meat. The ten second rule. Don't ya know it? Ya shoulda gone to college like your big sister," he looks up, grinning at me; his teeth covered in brown sauce. I can see the vestiges of meat stuck in his teeth, as he continues, chewing and speaking simultaneously. "Then you'd be all smart and at least know the frigging ten second rule. Right boys?" he rhetorically questions his two young sons, who just nod silently in return; anticipating a nasty escalation.

Jack shoots my sister another zinger. "You're fucking useless Pris, get me a beer. Can ya do that without dropping the fucking thing? At least, can ya manage that? And shut that kid up, will ya?" The baby screams louder now. Once again, Pris starts to move to the baby, wanting to follow his orders but with the hope that he'll stop his abusive demands.

"The beer! Are ya deaf?" he shakes a greasy rib in her face. Pris immediately obeys and gets the beer, brings it to Jack and makes another attempt to respond to her crying child.

I break in with, "Please, let me get the baby Pris." I go to the baby.

Jack instantly growls back, "Don't touch that kid Charlie. That's her job, ya got it?"

I stare back at him. I'd like to take that knife on the table and stick it deep inside his chest. I sit there and imagine Jack dropping to the floor dead; me knowing that I rescued my sister and him realizing how much I despise him. I jolt awake and sit up. I find it hard to breathe. Oh my god.

Chapter Eleven

HAVANA — THE MORNING AFTER

The dreams remain vivid as I pace the room. How did I ever desert those poor kids? What's wrong with me? What kind of big sister am I? I could see how traumatized those children were that night at dinner almost two years ago and yet again Pris' funeral. Why did I cut them off when they needed me? My head is full of nagging questions. My brother, why didn't he do something at the funeral? He's always so distant with family. I understand why. Our mother, an obsessive compulsive and controlling matriarch. Our father, disappearing from our lives when I was only six years old; flying the cuckoo's nest. He just couldn't endure another minute of the ups and downs of our bi-polar mother and instead chose to abandon his three young children. My brother Sam's foundational defense mechanism became his carefree, 'nothing really matters' approach to life which continues today. Sam's belief – no strings! No heavy relationships ever! No connection with Jack, his dysfunctional degenerate brother in law and yes, nor any association with Jack's kids. The most nagging question in my mind now - why did Jack treat Priscilla so badly? There is no question that Pris loved him, and was committed to him.

She was the nicest person; much nicer, kinder to others than either me or my brother put together. She was totally open to everyone, no matter what strata of society they represented. I envied her uninhibited view of the world. She loved people; and people were in turn, instantly drawn to her. But she was vulnerable and weak; and Jack knew that he could take advantage of Pris' kind heart – her unceasing desire to please anyone close to her.

It's morning in Havana. I can hear the rain outside the window, beating down on old town Havana. The humidity remains unbearable despite the pounding rain. My sheets are wet from sweat. My head is still in a fog. Must be the residual of the sedative. I go to the balcony, hover like the moth I see on the iron railing. The rain has seeped in from the open balcony door, and the drapes are drenched. The streets look slick, the buildings appear dirtier in the rain. Locals rush along the pavement on the way to work or someplace obviously demanding their immediate physical presence. The pedicabs below are full to the brim with bedraggled tourists, trying to escape the downpour.

I think back to last night. Disgusted. I am totally outraged with the sinister shenanigans I've had to deal with over the 24 hours. I yearn to exit this god forsaken country as soon as humanly possible, this time traveling without the special guidance from my number one enemy – Enrique Ruiz.

In my pit of despair, I pick up the blue velvet cloth and open it to gaze at the blue crystal given to me by Gurjot in Mexico; looking for some peace of mind or some insight to be uncovered. Nothing results. Instead, a surge of anger for both Enrique and Carla overtakes me; roaring through my veins.

"This crystal is useless Gurjot," I yell out to nobody. I am not the Brave One!" Enraged, I throw the crystal across the room. It lands on the antique rocking chair's seat cushion. I realize that I am, once again, in distress, almost worse than when I realized I had been kidnapped by that Cuban mongrel.

Then I notice that the chair does a little rock, at least three times back and forth, just after the small crystal lands on the padded cushion. I discount the absurd reaction of the chair. It's an inanimate object. At this moment, I hate the world in general.

Strangely enough, it dawns on me that although I long to be home, I have no desire to run to Doug who waits for me in Maui. I lack any emotional connection with Doug, my boyfriend, the one who consistently expresses his love for me. Love…love…only a foul four letter word. How the fuck did I think I was falling in love with the conniving Enrique Ruiz?

Even more puzzling, I wonder what is wrong with me that I am so easily deceived? Beguiled by a skilled human behaviorist who tricks rats using orchestrated positive and negative reinforcement. Enrique was the irresistible cheese. Both Carla and Enrique were the calculating masterminds of the wicked plot; targeted at producing a precise result from me – the ever-trusting rat. I won't do it! I won't participate in an illegal and dangerous undertaking just because these evil puppeteers are attempting to pull my strings. I won't succumb to that chunk of counterfeit cheese waiting for me in the rat maze. Screw them! Find another victim.

I spot the blue crystal on the chair's cushion and pick it up, apologizing in my mind to Gurjot. It's not your fault Gurjot. You told me to be brave. Now's the time for that! Now's the time! A burst of sunlight emerges through the clouds and shines into the room, hitting the blue crystal, and shooting hundreds of tiny flecks of lights on the walls. Stunned, I smile for a moment. For some reason, I can feel Priscilla around me in this crystal light shower. She loved to dance. I can see her dancing, arabesques across the room. I watch the lights shimmering on the furniture, on the bed, everywhere for just a few minutes, until the sun changes its position and the dance finishes. Priscilla fades away; melting out of the scene. Carefully, I wrap the crystal in the cloth and put it into my backpack which holds my camera.

I need a shower. I stink from that musty room where my abductors took me. I decide to wander the streets of Havana today. I need another 24 hours to recover from the drug and work through this depression, so I can travel with some confidence. After a luke warm shower, I notice that the rain has stopped, although the sky is still thick with heavy dark clouds. I feel like a zombie. My hair is frizzy, my body still weak. I feel dirty even after my shower; like the grit on the streets and buildings of Havana – hard to wash off.

A walk down to the famous Malécon and the old fort on the harbor would help me get back to normal. I don't want any breakfast; just not hungry. In the lobby, I realize that I didn't even bring my umbrella with me. I'm annoyed at my oversight.

Before I escape the hotel, a familiar voice shouts out from behind me. "Hola Charlie, you going out for a walk? It's supposed to rain again, so get your umbrella ready." It's Juan José. As I turn, I see that he has a giant pack of cigars in his hand. "Did your Cuban man smoke those things last night? Now you need some more of these kick ass cigars, si? Kick ass – you know like the San Francisco Giants."

He fakes batting a baseball with his cigar pack in hand. "Home run from Barry Bonds," he jokes, now making a crowd sound, clicking his tongue for a hit and cheering.

"So, you like baseball Juan Jose, yes?"

"Sí, my favorite sport, even better than soccer. If I weren't selling these cigars all the time, I would be at the baseball field hitting balls over the fence. Pow!" He gestures another home run. "You like this game too?" he asks, hoping I do.

"Me? Of course, I love baseball. I live near San Francisco. What do you think? I go to Giants games whenever I get the chance. I like sitting right behind home plate where I can get the best photographs and maybe even catch a foul ball."

He is pleased that I share his passion. "Wow. Where you going anyway? Charlie, you look kind of tired today," he says like my little big brother.

"I'm okay Juan, no worries. I'm going for a long walk."

"Sure," he nods. "Hey Charlie, I saw you last night in the café – right there with that big Cuban man. I was selling cigars to the Germans at the other table. You looked happy one minute, drinking your alcohol and then I see you get really tired.

I see you slump down and that man picked you up and helped you out. But then I see another man with a white hat follow you guys. Where you go? What happened to you? "

"Oh – ummm." What do I say to him? "I- I just had a sudden headache and I-I guess I was really tired. My friend just helped me back to my room so I could rest."

Juan doesn't seem to quite believe me but he politely drops the subject. He nods his head considering my story.

"You go to the Malécon, maybe now? I can go with you and guide you," he offers.

"Yes, I'm headed in that direction. But you're right. I'm not feeling so well today. I'm going to walk alone for awhile Juan. Maybe I'll see you down there."

He seems saddened by my gentle but clear rejection. "Okay Charlie. My sister, Marta is meeting me at the Malécon. I will leave here as soon as I sell four more boxes of cigars; so hope to see you there. Si? My sister has never met any Americans. And I don't see many here in Habana; so it's big deal for me. Maybe you buy more cigars later?" I give him a little hug.

"Maybe I will. See you Juan Jose, either down at the Malécon or back here later." I snap his photo as he stands there in the lobby of The Hotel Inglaterra. He holds up a box of supremo cigars and flashes his dimples. I don't much feel like laughing but he gives me several amusing poses and I just can't help but smile, even giggle a little. He sits on the sofa pretending to smoke. I snap his photo. He crosses his legs like a big macho Cuban man. I snap that one. He pretends he's a tourist standing in line for a room. I snap that one. He bats like Barry Bonds again. I snap that one. After about seven or eight photos, I wave goodbye. We have bonded through this spontaneous photo shoot.

As I walk away from the Hotel Inglaterra, the thought of Enrique abducting me and taking me just ten steps away floods back to me. I try to forget about it as I move through the Old Havana streets. I was clearly not in the mood to embark on a travel shoot when I groggily awoke this morning, but Juan José has helped to at least temporarily lift my dragging spirits. I think about photography and why I enjoy it so much. I like magical moments and capturing them with my camera. I read somewhere that the best shots are often achieved when the photographer has experienced an emotional trauma which can have a profound positive effect on your work. Facial expressions not found interesting before, the minor features of a crumbling building you may not have noticed otherwise, or the light on the sidewalk you thought no big deal and which you would ordinarily pass up. After a emotionally-charged experience, you may come alive in a whole new way as a photographer – have a breakthrough like any artist who goes through extreme pain or depression.

I notice how the rain has produced a slippery shimmering effect everywhere I look. The palm trees around the hotel have a silky patina. The tattered black iron fire escapes on the old tenement opposite my hotel room are glistening. The shot looking up from the pavement where I stand, through the line of fire escapes to the sky, is incredible. I stop walking, ease my camera from my back pack, aim and shoot straight up. I look ahead of me. About half a block away, I can see a tall skinny, very black Cuban woman walking towards me; her thin clothes look soaked from the rainstorm. She removes the wicker basket full of heavy sacks of grain from the top of her head and with her hands, attempts to scoop out the rain water which has collected in the straw receptacle. Some of the grain spills to the ground in a small heap. As she bends down to grab the sack, her colorful but tattered shawl falls to the pavement and into a large dirty puddle of water. She is definitely miffed, privately cursing aloud to herself in response to her hairy predicament. I am automatically shooting each slice of this candid street scene, using my auto zoom. Click, click, click. Each click features the contrast of her beauty and the mess she's got on her hands. By the time I reach her and walk by, she has everything organized and together; and now appears to not have a care in the world.

I stroll by the incredibly beautiful and immense colonial white Hotel Nacional, previously described by Enrique only yesterday; before I knew him like I know him now. Before he became my enemy. Taking in my surroundings, I can see why this was the government's palace of power. It's like the grand splendor of the decadent 1940's and 50's is ostentatiously rolled out before my eyes. What emperor would not want to reside here? You can feel the power of the structure as you enter through the elaborate, heavy doors. When the pompous but polite door attendant opens the palatial door for me, I nod in appreciation and walk into a stunning grand lobby. He thinks I'm one of his precious hotel guests, I am sure.

The majesty of the ceilings, walls and floors are dazzling to the eye. The black granite reception desk goes on forever. I walk by the main dining room which is colossal; the clanking of expensive silver trays and antique coffee pots command my attention. People wait to be seated and served – all dressed to the nines for a grand brunch. I can see the buffet tables piled high with fruits, cakes and pastries of every imaginable size, shape, color and decoration. I can't remember when I've seen such a luxurious spread of stunning food in one place.

The bell men and waiters are impeccably outfitted in uniforms resembling officers of some first class Navy; draped with gold cords, epaulets of dark blue fringe adorning their jackets made of pricey deep burgundy fabric. They rush around helping rich tourists with their bags, pushing elegant gold carts of Louis Vuitton and Tumi suitcases to and from elevators, holding mink coats in their regimented arms; each one hoping to get a fat tip for their services. The piped in hotel music I hear as I walk through the Hotel Naciõnal is none other than my favorite - Bésame Mucho; except not mariachi style this time but instead a dignified orchestral rendition. I prefer the mariachis. Charlie, wake up - you are not in Mexico anymore.

I photograph a uniformed bell man who appears picture perfect; but sports a soured facial expression as he turns away from just receiving an evidently underweight tip from a fat over-dressed European woman. I snap the scene with my Nikon from yards away; capturing his disappointment. He doesn't even notice me. He rushes to assist another tourist in need; hopeful once again. As I decide to exit the hotel, I can't help but ask myself one question. How can there be so many rich people in here and so many struggling Havana locals out there? I know it happens in many cities around the world but it never ceases to amaze me. Cuba – a culture of contradictions. I could see the poverty right outside my own middle class Hotel Inglaterra – kids in rags, homeless people milling about. The Hotel Nacioñal, the behemoth of elegant hotels takes the class contrast to a whole new level; highlighting the 'haves and have nots' in Havana.

I find my way through the streets to the Malécon near the city's harbor area. People stroll down this walkway as if enjoying the left bank of the Seine. It's an atmosphere of hustle; locals desperately trying to make a fast buck from European, South American and Asian tourists. They offer a variety of products – cheap jewelry, watches, scarves, toys and a other oddball trinkets. You name it!

What strikes me the most are the services offered literally in the same spot - prostitutes, like peacocks with their multi-colored make-up, clad in skimpy clothes; dozens of them hanging out by the center stone fountain at the sea wall. Very young faces; some pretty and others not so blessed physically. Their youth is what is astounding. Some look only thirteen or fourteen years old. They strut about advertising their services on this early afternoon amidst children, babies, elderly people. The tourists stare at the prostitutes. The locals appear numbed to this tableau. One by one, the prostitutes approach each man, whether with or without a woman at their side. There is no separation… no divide in this town between red light district activities and the ordinary bustle of people taking a leisurely mid-day walk.

My camera takes over as if I am merely the robot operator. Facial expressions, provocative and spontaneous scenes now preserved in time from street vendors, tourists, locals and those prostitutes. Unforgettable images surround me. A photographic booty found here. Opposite the stone wall is a long row of upscale mini mansions, each house different than the next in color and style. What a contrast with these prostitutes across the street clothed in mini skirts, short shorts – a latex extravaganza.

I block out Enrique and Carla; and get lost playing with my camera, by far my favorite toy. After about an hour of photography, I plunk my body on the steps of the stone wall not far from the parade of young prostitutes. Taking out the map of the city I picked up earlier from the concierge at my hotel, I consider where I might walk next in this city.

"Charlie, hey Charlie, over here." I can hear Juan's voice from behind me. He runs towards me and sits down next to me.

"Hola, Juan." He sees me with map in hand.

"Charlie, you maybe walk to the fortress down there," he points to the right. I see a beautiful dirty white, almost brownish structure, sitting out on the harbor's point.

"Great suggestion." Juan waves to a young woman who holds a small baby and smiles brightly. "That is my sister Marta over there and her niño, Jovi, only three months old. He is named after Bon Jovi, you know, the American singer. Of course, you know him."

"Yes, I like his music."

Juan rises and then gestures like he is Bon Jovi playing his music, tossing his head around energetically and yanking on his imaginary guitar strings. I point at Juan with my camera, silently asking if he can please re-create that rock star pose for the pleasure of me and my Nikon. Juan instantly obliges, going into action with even more zest than the first time. Click, click, click. Sitting back down beside me, Juan confides, "I will take care of little Jovi today for Marta. She works here all day at the Malécon on Saturdays."

I am flabbergasted by what Juan has just disclosed to me. Numerous questions flash through my mind. First, is Marta actually one of the prostitutes? She seems to be hanging out with these other teenage girls who are obviously engaged in selling their bodies for cash. And how old is Marta? She appears to be barely in her mid teens, if that. And this pretty young Marta has a baby? Somehow it all seems normal down here on the Malécon.

I get my courage up and inquire further, "So Juan, your sister works here with the other girls?" Si, she is a prostitute, a whore. We call them the "las prostitutas" in Havana. Marta sells her body for sex to the tourists. She make a lot of dollars here. But she also work five days a week at the cigar factory in Pinar del Río. Mi madre watch Jovi most of the time while Marta work alot. But today, they ask me to do it. No worry, I will work tonight at The Inglaterra and sell more cigars. Saturday night, so business should be muy bueno."

I dare to dig a little deeper with Juan. "Marta is so lovely. How old is she Juan?" "She's a woman now, almost 15 years old with her birthday next month. She trying to make a lot of money and save all of it." Then Juan breaks into a soft whisper, "She want to go to America with Jovi, but you need a lot of money to give to the guys who can get you out of Cuba. They are the underground guys, you know what I mean? You see that area out in the open sea? That sharp rock area by that harbor right over there?" He points. "Sí, sí? They go off in little boats trying to make it to Miami; but they get caught or die trying to get there on some small no good boat. My cousin, he die trying to get to Florida on a rubber dingy boat – stupido! Marta will do it in more safe way. I give her some of my cigar money to help her save faster and…"

His words are cut off by Marta yelling from where she stands with her parading colleagues. "Juan, hey Juan. Ven aca." She waves for him to come over. "Lo siento Charlie, look like Marta have her first customer. German guy, I think. Ugly and fat." Juan laughs. "See you later."

He rises and starts to sprint to Marta. Turning now Juan runs backwards still at a brisk pace He yells back to me, "Hey Charlie, you look better than when I see you first this morning. I go to watch Jovi at my house now. Hey - you should walk to La Punta, the old fortress. You will like it." He mimes me shooting photos with my camera and points in the direction of the sprawling white fortress; then turns to Marta and rushes to her. I see Marta quickly hand off the baby to her brother. Juan takes the baby and walks away as a tall thin Cuban man wearing a black fedora, dark sunglasses and a black raincoat takes money from a hefty European-looking man. The Cuban taps Marta on the shoulder, signaling her to go with the client.

The newly acquainted pair head off down the street in the direction of old Havana. Another young prostitute, even younger than Marta passes right in front of me, arm in arm with an aging Italian-looking client. He is already caressing the girl's round bottom as they stroll by, warming up for their impending sexual romp. I pretend to be shooting the harbor with my camera, but instead I click away at the couple, capturing the client's lecherous facial expressions and his large hand on her butt as he pinches and massages, then pinches it again. She feigns delight with several forced giggles. Click, click, click. Yes, I think, that man certainly got himself a very pretty prostitute here in Havana town. He looks pleased, even proud like a rooster about to pounce on a fenced-in hen. Geez.

I guess the sex industry is the one thing that Fidel Castro cannot ration. I watch the girl and her client walk away. That girl has no childhood, just like Marta. Her teenage years will never exist with high school parties or proms or lying to your parents or even telling a little white lie to your parents about studying at a friend's house when you are really hanging out with your teen boyfriend. There are no lies here; down at the Malécon. I sit and wonder what will happen to these girls as they get older. How will they end up? I wish I could help kids who are in trouble. They need advocates, people who can support them and guide them in a constructive direction.

Sadness consumes me as I walk down the Malécon, thinking about heading to the fortress. I think of Theresa, the little baby from last night and her mother now being treated for cancer in a Miami hospital. Will Theresa ever feel the arms of her mother again? Will she grow up without becoming a prostitute in Havana? The skies open up on the water's edge. It starts to rain. No umbrella, no rain gear; not even a hat or sweater.

I'd better get back to the hotel versus risk getting waterlogged with a long walk to the fortress. My passion for shooting street scenes with my Nikon seems to have faded. I drag myself back; the rain beating down on me. I lift my backpack up over my head in an attempt to shield the downpour. My hair already hangs like a mop, large drips of precipitation from the tenement fire escapes and overhangs now trickle down my back. I glance at my cheap pale blue Mexican blouse purchased from the Cancun marketplace, and see it is now totally transparent from the rain, all the details of my animal print bra now visible to all of Havana. What I must look like to the locals.

Chapter Twelve

OLD HAVANA — MY ABOUT FACE

S oaked to the bone, I now find myself close to The Hotel Inglaterra. Crying as the rain pours down, my body is drenched with guilt and sorrow; my heart still crushed from Enrique's betrayal. I had more than trust for him. I was falling in love. I thought our connection was magical; almost surreal. How inept could I have been? Somehow the rain beating down on me now feels like therapy; providing a welcome release, a sort of cleansing of the body and soul. Instead of rushing into the hotel lobby to face the discomfort of being sopping wet in a suddenly dry place, I turn and cross the street to the park which is empty of both tourists and locals. No children running about, no elders taking afternoon walks, no Europeans feverously licking melting ice cream cones in the hot afternoon sun. Only me sitting alone on a weathered wooden bench in a serious rainstorm.

I drift to thoughts of Priscilla and recall the last conversation I ever had with my sister. It was only two days before the end of her life. Once I knew how emotionally unstable she was, I encouraged Pris to call my 800 number any day, any time, any hour. She would call me regularly at least once or twice a week, always during the daytime. When she phoned me that very last time, I was tired. My morning loaded with client calls and pitch planning with Doug. I had been in the midst of drafting a complex presentation for a hot potential new client; trying to muster as much personal creativity as I possibly could to beat our competitors on the project. Pris called me just as I was wrapping up, developing the presentation summary that I was hoping would clinch the deal. As soon as I heard her voice, I knew that Pris was in cataclysmic emotional shape. She talked of objects falling on her head. She talked of car after car hitting her head-on, describing the impact and destruction to her physical body. I listened in shock. My first inclination was to use logic to prove that she was really okay. She's alive and talking to me, isn't she? Nothing has hit her. I wanted to convince her with my rational and practical reasoning; have her see reality.

When she told me that she was sitting in her bathroom as were speaking. I asked her to please look in the mirror.

"Pris, do you see yourself in that mirror?"

Her response, "Yes, I look terrible." I continued with this approach, desperate, not knowing any other track to take.

"So, you are physically fine then, right Pris? You are standing and looking at yourself, my pretty sister, in your mirror. What are you wearing?"

She laughs. "White blouse, blue pants, messy hair." I think maybe I've broken through. She's managing for now. "And there is no blood anywhere - right?" I ask to insure there is nothing else going on.

"You're right Charlie, I see myself in the mirror and like you said, I'm okay. Silence for some moments. "But what's wrong with me?" What the hell is going on with me?" She breaks down on the phone. Why do I keep feeling like I'm dying, being killed? I can't help it! I-l just can't help it! Sometimes, I want...." I cut her off right there. "Listen, Pris. You're fine!"

And then she sabotages herself with the cycle repeating all over again. She goes into describing another vehicle hitting her. Only this time it's a large truck, then a heavy painting hanging from her wall, crashing onto her head, knocking her out and finally killing her. Then she's in her back yard and wild animals are ripping her to shreds. I could barely keep up with the horrific things she described to me, all happening one right after the other. We went around in circles that day on the phone. Me, using the logic card and her, agreeing to my sober rationale; then immediately coming up with yet another morbid hallucination. Priscilla's hell!

After about an hour into our call, Pris was close to collapse from emotional exhaustion and then announced that she needed to go; get off the phone. Through her sobbing, she said, "The baby is awake, screaming for me, and the boys will be home any minute. I'd better go now."

I didn't want to hang up. I asked her if she were seeing her psychiatrist regularly.

"Yes, I was going to Dr. Graham a couple of times a week, but it's so far to drive Charlie, and Jack can't take me any more because of his job. I need to be home for the kids anyway. It's just too much trouble with everything. Plus, Jack comes home late.

H-he didn't come home for two nights in a row a few days ago." She struggled to get that last statement out. This made me worry even more, if that were possible.

Out of any words of wisdom, I wished Pris a good night's sleep tonight, but in my heart I was panicking. I told her to call me any time; day or night. What could I do? I was 3000 miles away. I quickly called Jack. I had his work number. Although I never got to know him very well, I wanted to tell him that I was really worried about his wife; hoping to get his thoughts and reactions.

"Yeah," he answered the phone with complete annoyance. When I shared my concerns about Pris, he responded with, "There's nothing wrong with her. She's only fakin' it. Hell, she's lucky I even come home most nights. Your sister's not mentally ill Charlie. She's bluffing and just lazy now since she's got three kids instead of two. Shit! It's me, her goddamn husband, that's goin' nuts. I'm the victim here – not Pris Miss. Look - I gotta go now. It's been a real pleasure."

Shutting down the conversation with his sardonic tone, he hung up on me. I couldn't believe what I heard from Jack, this man who vowed to honor and respect my sister. Neither honor nor respect were part of his behavior or his vocabulary with regard to anybody. I was trembling like a leaf after the call. Quickly, I got my brother on the phone, giving him the rundown of my previous two conversations. Sam was more lucid than I at this point. He suggested that we take a trip to Florida, spend some time with Pris and the kids, take them away for a mini holiday, then look into her medical situation. We could spend a week there. He said that he would call Pris the next morning, check in and settle on the date for us to travel. The next morning finally arrived. Sam followed through and called Pris. Jack answered the phone. It was too late. She was dead!

"Gassed herself in our fuckin' Toyota hatchback," Jack exploded to Sam. When my brother called me to break the news, before he said a word, I knew Pris was dead. I don't know how or why – but I knew it. Maybe it was Sam's belabored breathing which I noticed at the moment I picked up the phone. Maybe I heard his throat choke up right before he said, "Charlie, I have some bad news about Pris."

Here, on this park bench in Old Havana, my tears flow, as if I just got off the phone with Sam; as if he just spilled the tragic news all over me like the rain beating down on me now. I failed Pris, I failed those kids, and basically I've failed myself. I lacked courage. How can I be the brave one? What was Gurjot thinking? Was he blind? I look up at the hotel just across from the park and notice a scraggly dog romping through a muddy puddle, then vigorously shaking the water from his undernourished body. To shake off my own guilt, I'm ready to help children out of troubled situations. I know I want to do this in my life going forward. There are lots of kids in need out there.

A wave of clarity rushes over me as I experience a personal paradigm shift.

I stare straight ahead through the falling raindrops. It's Enrique. I see him walk out of the dilapidated building only steps away from the Hotel Inglaterra; the same building where

I was his hostage. He's heading this way crossing through the park. Even from a distance, my heart can't help but take a leap. Even now, after everything! For some reason, my anger for this man has subsided. He doesn't see me yet. He pulls his jacket over his head for some protection from the weather. It's still raining hard. The puddles are expanding everywhere I look. I break into a run; racing to Enrique, sprinting across the squishy park lawn, my back pack dragging on the ground. "Enrique, Enrique." I catch my breath and grab onto his sleeve.

"Charlie, qué pasa? You are soaking wet. Come, let's go inside and get you dry."

I tug him again to stop and listen. "Wait Enrique. I will do it! I know I'm crazy; but I need to do it. I need to do something really generous for once in my life. I will help little Theresa and take her to Miami to see her mother again."

He starts to talk, say something. I shut him up with a long, wet kiss. He embraces me and embellishes the kiss with full force and affection. Then he sprinkles tiny kisses across the bridge of my dripping wet nose. He laughs and twirls me around.

"Gracias, Miss Charlotte Sweeney. You are my family's special angel from above." He looks deep into my eyes. "But you know this is risky, sí? Are you ready to take such a risk?"

"Yes, I am."

"Are you clear that we will not be able to talk ever again after you hand off little Theresa in Miami? Any linkage between us will be much too risky for you and for me, my family.

"Yes, Enrique. I understand."

Taking his hand in mine, I lead him back through the park to The Hotel Inglaterra, into the elevator and up to Room 324.

Chapter Thirteen

THE BEGINNING OF OUR END

Love comes around the corner so fast, like a dear friend you haven't seen for a long time, showing up in a place you never expected; even in a foreign country. I remember being in Paris several years ago at the Musee D'Orsay, mesmerized by the circular Monet mural room I was standing in, surrounded by those vivid and life-like water lilies from Giverny. Squealing with delight, my Aunt Helen at my side, we admired the beautiful work of art. As I turned with pleasure, laughing out loud, I found myself suddenly face to face with my best friend from college – Jenny Paddington. She appeared out of nowhere. I hadn't seen Jenny for years since Queens College, New York City. What were the chances we'd meet in Paris or ever meet again after being so totally out of touch for so many years? She had moved to Paris. And it was her birthday the day we re-connected; a serendipity beyond belief. Like the surprise of Jenny in that French museum, I now find sudden deep passionate love. I didn't start my journey to Cuba expecting anything like this. I was happy with Doug; one of the nicest men to ever enter my life. But here with Enrique, I have hit the mother lode; uncovering an overflowing gold mine of sweet love and affection. Our physical connection will, most likely, be fleeting - but our spiritual link is another story. We won't have a fairy tale ending. I may even get thrown in jail. Despite this, the quality time I spend in Room 324 with Enrique will nurture me with happiness for the rest of my life.

It's a waste of time to try and describe how he touches my body; or to elaborate on the electricity ignited between us, the flame triggered when we unite as one. If I think about it too much, it may lose its potency; cheapen the limited moments we have together. All I can say is that tonight I am wrapped in the warm blanket of this man. He is like the lavender cologne I can't wait to put on my body every day. His scent intoxicates me.

I am now officially unfaithful to Doug. I am sorry for this; but Doug is not Enrique. They have no resemblance to one another; and, in some ways, they are literally two direct opposites. After we make love here in Room 324, we hold each other for several hours into the early morning.

Enrique whispers. "It's love Charlie. Let's not make believe it's something else even though we know that our time together is short. We could pretend that this is only sexual or that the night we just spent together had no meaning; or that this is my way of keeping you convinced that you should take the little baby back to her madre. There will be no pretending for us. Sí, my love?"

I start to say something, but Enrique touches my lips with his fingers,

"Shhh," he says, his eyes locked with mine. "I love you Charlie. Please, no need to tell me in return, just feel my heart bonded to yours like a magnet. I did not mean to fall in love with you. But I am far beyond just *falling* in love. I cherish you Charlie, ever since I made our accidental collision possible at San Francisco Airport. The moment I looked into your ocean blue eyes, I began to fall."

For an hour or so, there is quiet between us, as we cling together in peace - both having lost valuable things and people in our lives; but now finding each other.

Waking to the morning sun shining through the balcony window, I see that Enrique is sitting on the rocking chair. He slowly rocks. When he sees me move, he smiles as he holds up two cups of coffee and a cellophane bag of what looks like pastries. "Good morning. The day is beautiful, Charlie. I already have our breakfast." He brings it over to me, gently inviting me to take a bite of a delicious almond pastry. I'm evidently ravenous.

"What happens now?" I ask him.

"We start your education. You must learn everything about your new fake persona. Miguel will be your teacher."

Did he say Miguel? "Miguel, your cousin from Cancun?"

"Sí, Miguel is much more than a restaurant proprietor and chef. He is part of the underground here in Cuba – going back and forth from Cancun to Habana. He hates Castro almost as much as I do. He is really my ex-brother-in-law, Charlie."

Enrique sits down next to me on the big brass bed. "I was married for six years to a beautiful and very outspoken Cuban woman; what I believe you call - brazen . Her name was Rita; and she was Miguel's younger sister." Enrique gets up and paces the room; then settles on the rocking chair again. As he rocks, Enrique spills his terrible tale.

"On an ordinary day, just like today, Rita was caught purchasing red meat on the black market. Red meat… it was illegal for Cubans to have red meat…only for tourists and important government officials. Castro was even rationing our daily rice, bread and beans. Devil!" Disgusted when he speaks of Castro, Enrique grimaces. " It was the birthday of Rita's father. He was turning 60 years old. She wanted to please him and planned a surprise dinner for the whole family in honor of his birthday. She bought five beefsteaks from a black marketer right here on the street. It was a trick; undercover citizens paid to entice people to buy the food banned for purchase - like beefsteaks. She was caught… sentenced to three years in prison. Prison for buying some red meat!" He yells this out.

I close the balcony door so his shouts won't be heard to cause attention. His story shakes me; so different than the world I live in and take for granted. After last night, I didn't think anything else would surprise me. Enrique drops his head in sorrow. I can see, that like me, he is still grieving.

Enrique continues in a solemn tone. "One visiting day I arrived at the prison. The guard came out to talk to me." He pauses and swallows hard, "but without Rita. He tells me that my wife is dead. My Rita – dead! Died from a sudden brain hemorrhage in her sleep. All I could see in front of me was Castro's head severed from his body. El Diablo!" Enrique weeps now. The rocking chair stops.

I am very quiet. After some minutes, he sits up limply in the chair. I sip my coffee. The tears well up in my eyes. I move over to his chair and sit down on my knees before him.

"What can I say Enrique...except... I know what it's like to suddenly lose someone you love."

"I see. I am sorry." He strokes my hair.

"Yes, my sister Priscilla committed suicide about a year ago... leaving her three young children behind. He looks up at me with surprise and then with sincere sympathy. This is followed by a long, understanding quiet between us.

"We are both broken in a similar way," he says. "Our paths were meant to cross, si? Even if this collision was managed through my clever cousin Carla. Meeting you is a very fortunate event for my family...and for me Charlie." He kisses the top of my head, sweeps the long hanging curls from my face; then slides down to the damp tiled floor and holds me in his close embrace.

"I must go now. Miguel is here with mi madre. I must see him; tell him that you you've changed your mind and will take Theresa to Miami."

I kiss him softly on his lips. He continues, "Your education must start today. Miguel will be your teacher. He will prepare you with your new identity. Are you okay to begin your training?"

I hesitate, thinking that this process must be quite organized. I guess I didn't quite internalize that before now. I say, "Yes, yes Enrique, I'm ready to learn everything about my new identity."

"If you agree, it will take place in the same loft I took you before - just steps away from this hotel. Can you find your way to that building?

"Yes, I'm sure I can.   "Just knock four times and I will open the door. Please be sure to knock four times exactly. Sí?"

I nod. He kisses me on my forehead like I am his sweet child and he is leaving me so that I can get on the school bus, but promises me with his eyes that he will see me later.

I am left alone in my hotel room. I sit in the rocking chair with the blue crystal in my hand. The sun catches the gem once again, and flecks of light jump and dance on the wall before me. I whisper out into nowhere, but I know Priscilla is listening, "Pris, I will help little Theresa be with her mother again. You are my inspiration. I love you. Please guide me through this challenge of a lifetime."

Chapter Fourteen

HAVANA — A NEW IDENTITY

If I admit to myself that my nerves have now taken over my entire body, I may decide to rescind my generous and maybe foolish offer to the Ruiz family. I try to think positively. Be the brave one! I can hear Gurjot saying this to me as I enter the abandoned building. I climb the dark, shadowed staircase and am careful to knock exactly four times on the scoffed green door. Enrique greets me with his warm and thankful smile. He takes my hand leading me into the room. We are alone.

Sitting down at the table, he says, "Miguel will be here soon, but some words of caution – he is tough Charlie. He can be rough. This training may be too much for you. Please remember, you can change your mind at any time." I shake my head.

"No Enrique, my commitment is solid. It will not waver. I must…" I am cut off by a knock two times at the door. Two times only. Shouldn't it be four times like me? Isn't that the code? Then - two more knocks. Enrique looks over at me and puts his forefinger to his lips.

"Shh," he whispers. Have the Cuban authorities already discovered our planned criminal act? Shit, I'm nervous - shaking. The knocking goes silent. A few moments later, knocking again. This time – four sequential knocks. Then nothing. Enrique is waiting, not moving. Four knocks again but somehow seem to be coming from a lower area on the door; not where you'd usually knock.

Enrique moves to open the door; but I see that behind his back, he holds a knife, a switchblade of some sort. Shit, a knife. He moves quickly to the left side of the door and gestures me to come and stand next to him. I instantly obey. He flings open the door, and Miguel is sprawled out on the floor, outside the door, attempting to gather up his things from the grimy stone floor: papers, a briefcase, a sack with something heavy inside.

"Mierdé, Mierdé!" he snarls at us like a savage dog.

"Qué pasa Miguel?" Enrique is relieved. He helps Miguel to stand up. "Miguel is not quite as agile as most Cubans." Enrique bursts out laughing. "You're an old man, sí?"

Miguel tries to pull Enrique to the floor with him, then wrestles him to the ground. He sees me in the doorway now. They both gather Miguel's things into the room and close the door behind them.

"What are you carrying, my cousin? Why the big load?"

"I tripped on the damn steps. Too many stairs for a man of my size. This building is a pigsty and a danger to a large man like me. I must complain to the government – to Fidel Castro," he laughs sarcastically. "This will cost you more now Enrique," he teases. "How about a bottle of whiskey between us before we start her education? Do you have any? Ahh – no worries cousin - I have a big bottle with me here in my bag."

He pulls out the bottle; which fortunately hasn't broken from the back pack having fallen to the floor. I'm wondering now if Miguel is the right guy to train me for this dangerous mission. Does he really know what to do to prepare me?

"Ok cousin, one drink then." Enrique pats him on the back. Miguel produces three drinking glasses and a large bottle of brown alcohol.

"Looks like whiskey." Enrique smiles with appreciation.

"Oh no, not for me, no whiskey for me. Thanks anyway," I say. Then I realize that this is an opportunity to drive home an important point with these two Cubans. "I think I had enough to drink last night with *that mojito* – don't you?" I respond sarcastically.

Miguel raises his eyebrows and grabs me for one of his signature bear hugs. He laughs. "That cousin of mine drugged you with a mojito, sí? I heard all about it. It's true; it was my idea. But I promise, I am not really a brute like Enrique may have described. Trust me. You must have some whiskey before we start, si? Come on. I will not take your refusal on this, Charlie."

Miguel sits me back down and smacks the glass hard down on the table. "You need to get loosened up before you learn at lightening speed."

Enrique pours whiskey for all three of us. Miguel downs his drink in one quick gulp. Enrique takes his time enjoying every drop. I take a sip. It burns my throat and hits my stomach like a hot bullet.

"Wow," I blurt out. They both chuckle, amused by my amateur's reaction.

"Have a little more Charlie; just a little," Enrique directs me gently, assuring me that it is safe. "Not like the mojito," he promises. I drink again; this time a sizable sip. I feel like I need it. Who knows how this education session will go.

"Now down to business," Miguel declares. "You are Nicole Ann Marie McCoy Sparrow. Please say your name," he demands. "Sit up tall and say your new name with confidence. No more Charlie, no more Charlotte Sweeney, si?"

I am apprehensive, but I obey and say, "I am Nicole McCoy Sparrow."

"No, no, say the whole thing like it's nothing for you – Nicole Ann Marie McCoy Sparrow. Do it!" Miguel commands me.

I can see he has that caustic side, in great contrast to his Mexico head chef/restauranteur persona. Maybe he should lay off the whiskey, I think to myself. "Nicole Ann Marie McCoy." I manage to get it out fully – no gaps. "Nicole Ann Marie McCoy," I say again with increased confidence.

"Sparrow," he barks. "Sí? Nicole Ann Marie McCoy Sparrow."

Geez, I think, "why use such a long name?"

We walk through my newly assigned birth date, my birth place, my birth mother, father's name, my sibling's names, where

I grew up and my husband's name. My husband is Lucas Sparrow, singer and leader of a rock band called Sparrow. Like I would ever be married to a rock star. Evidently, Sparrow just played a gig in Havana and also in a place called Varadero. I travelled with Lucas, my husband, here to Cuba along with my baby, Lisa Ann Marie McCoy. That should not be too difficult to remember. More information. I also was a singer, but when I got serious with Lucas, I stopped performing. We married and started our family with Lisa Ann Marie. Shit! A lot to remember. More and more little details I need to know backwards and forwards cascade out from Miguel's mouth; hitting me with a new data point about once every minute.

Then he goes back to the very beginning and has me go through the whole thing from the start with the first detail – my new name. He takes out a small chalkboard from his bag, which he can erase as we go along. He has me write on the back and front of this small board as he quizzes me. This goes on for a couple of hours.

"Your name?" I write it. "Your birth date?"

I write that. Every detail, I write it. I make mistakes on Lisa's birth date and birth place. Miguel is not pleased with my errors.

"No, it is Fields Hospital in Ventura, California. That is the birthplace. Please – again I will ask you." He admonishes me more and more as he downs slug after slug of his hard whiskey.

"Where did your husband play concerts in Cuba?

"Vara…vara. Geez, I don't know. What is that place again?" I ask.

"Varadera! Varadera – a beach resort. Here, let me write it." He raises his voice again. Come on – remember everything! Everything!"

Enrique breaks in, "Miguel, stop! She needs a rest."

"One minute. One more minute, cousin," he insists. "Let's get it right first. Would you rather she gets sent to Habana prison, like your dead wife?"

Shocked, I look at Enrique. "It's okay," he says to me. I guess he's used to this behavior from his cousin; and he accepts it.

Miguel writes Varadera on the board and firmly places it close to my face. Then he erases it.

"Now, you write it – where did Lucas play his music in Cuba?"

I write Varadera and Old Havana. "How many concerts? he demands"

Three, I write; two in Old Havana and one in Varadera. I say this as I write it.

"Bien. Bien."

Miguel smiles; then paces the room. He takes another slug of whiskey. "Where is your husband now Mrs. Nicole Ann Marie McCoy Sparrow? Where is your husband Lucas now?"

Did he already tell me where my husband is and I don't remember. "I-I don't know." I put my head down on the table. I'm exhausted and hot. I don't have a towel or anything to wipe my dripping forehead.

"That's right – you don't know because I haven't told you yet," he shouts as he laughs and drinks more whiskey. Enrique stands behind me, rubbing my shoulders, supporting me as I'm grilled by this large, unpredictable and very drunk Cuban man.

"Stop, stop," Miguel yells at me. He slams the blackboard onto the floor. "No more chalkboard, no more writing. I want you to tell me everything about your new identity - all that you can remember. Go ahead - start from the top. No mistakes now, it is too expensive and it will cost you. Think of it as big money. You screw up and it costs you millions – maybe your life. Comprendes?" He lowers his voice and moves his chair next to me. "But first - please have another little drink, sí? We drink together to your new identity." He pours more and clinks glasses with me. I take another sip, now starting to enjoy the burning liquid.

He gestures for me to stand up and begin. I spew out the details starting from the basic information. I go on for almost thirty minutes and end with the fact that Lucas was on a visiting arts visa to Cuba. My daughter, Lisa Marie got sick with an ear infection. She couldn't fly; but Lucas needed to be back in Florida where he has three more gigs. I stayed behind until the baby recovered over the last three days. Now, I am flying back home to join him in Miami, for his final tour gigs in Florida - before we travel back home to California together. Miguel stands up and applauds me. He reaches into his beat-up rucksack and throws two passports, two airline tickets and a large box of disposable Cuban baby diapers, onto the rickety table.

"I knew you were beautiful, but not this smart! You have absorbed all of it, every detail. Bravo." He starts applauding again; then falls to the floor in his drunkenness, guffawing with delight. "You think I'm drunk? This is nothing! Nothing!" Enrique shrieks with delight at his cousin's success and gives me his own round of applause.

"Okay, you are ready to leave tomorrow for Miami, sí?" Miguel stares me in the face. Enrique abruptly stops his laughing.

"What do you mean Miguel? Tomorrow is too soon. Why the rush? I thought Charlie could stay for a few more days so she can feel…"

Miguel interrupts, "Impossible cousin. The longer we wait – the more risky! U.S. Customs is putting in new guidelines. I just learned this. More scrutiny on entries from Cuba – American or not. More formal regulations coming any day. We can't wait! I don't recommend stalling."

Enrique protests, No Miguel, I cannot…"

This time, I cut Enrique off. I feel loose now with the alcohol in my body and frankly, I'm annoyed. "Excuse me, but since you are both talking about me – I'd like to say something. Si?" They both turn to me.

"Sí". Enrique nods. "Of course Charlie – it's a woman's perog…perogatory to…"

"Stop." I laugh. I am still amused by his distortion of the English language. "Enrique, the expression is, it's a woman's pre-rogative to change her mind. Geez, you really need some comprehensive English lessons. Sorry, I won't be able to oblige with my departure. And no, I am not changing my mind. I will go tomorrow if that's what is necessary. It's probably better so I don't have too much time to forget the details of my new identity. Sí Miguel?"

Miguel sits back amused by my bravery. He seems impressed by me, "Si, you are brave too! I like that in a woman." he admits; my proud teacher - satisfied with the student whom he has taken from idiot to expert. I am now duly educated, ready to tackle anything – even baby smuggling. I am the brave one or am I really just a senseless, delusional and naïve woman in love?

 Four knocks on the door. I shoot Enrique a sharp glance, questioning him with my eyes. Who is that? Miguel rushes to the door and Doña Lia, Enrique's elderly mother enters, holding little Theresa; who squirms in her arms.

Relieved, Miguel speaks. "Charlie, you need to get to know your baby now, little Lisa Marie. You must take her with you tonight – get comfortable with her. Sleep with her by your side. The plane leaves at noon tomorrow on Habana Air. Miguel takes me by the shoulders. "I ask you one more time. Are you ready?"

Enrique takes the baby from his mother. The old woman cries out, tears streaming down her wrinkled cheeks as she strokes little Theresa's back and lets her go, "Niña. Mi niña!" She looks tired and scared for the baby's safety. Doña Lia takes my hand, kissing it over and over again. "Gracias Angel. Gracias."

Miguel has collapsed from exhaustion on the cot and has fallen fast asleep. He starts snoring but the drink, opening his eyes and catching himself when Theresa begins to cry. She does not want to leave her grandmother. My heart aches to see them about to be separated; but the love of your own birth mother is more compelling than staying with your grandma. I stand there visualizing a beautiful young woman praying and hopeful that someday she will touch her child again. I am anxious to achieve my goal; but am honestly dreading the process of getting to Miami.

Chapter Fifteen

DESTINATION MIAMI — TO BE OR NOT TO BE

It is my last night in Havana. I sit on the antique rocking chair, looking out through the wrought iron balcony, while the baby sleeps in my arms. I rock back and forth, listening to Theresa breathing, watching her petite face; her lips puckered up, perhaps dreaming of the future with her mama. I feel content; gratified to have this opportunity to help a family I've quickly come to love, in such a short time. Am I healed from being sedated by a man I was falling in love with, a man who makes my skin sizzle when he barely touches me? No – not totally healed, but I've already forgiven him. As I rock Theresa, I look over at this man now as he takes an afternoon nap on my hotel room bed, probably exhausted from a tough couple of days for both of us; maybe regretting this whole fiasco now set in high speed motion. Today, I could see how conflicted he was as Miguel was hammering in my new identity. Quiet now. Very quiet in this little oasis, tucked away here in The Hotel Inglaterra.

I close my eyes holding the baby tight and sense how it must feel to be a mother; the pride, the unconditional love, the protective instinct you must experience every waking minute of your life once your baby is born. I barely know this child, but I feel a heavy responsibility to get this child to Miami; if I make it. It's late afternoon when Theresa starts to move in my arms, suddenly wide awake and wanting to play. Her squeeze toy doesn't seem to please her. I reach over to my back pack and take out Gurjot's crystal, wrapped in the deep blue velvet cloth. Holding up the crystal in my hand, I can see the color almost matches Theresa's baby blue eyes. She is going to be a stunning girl and grow into a very pretty young woman; with her dark Cuban skin, her turquoise blue eyes and her silky blonde curly hair. Those little eyes are glued to watching the crystal as I move it up and down, back and forth. The sun catches it and produces dozens of large blue flecks that seem to dance on the printed wall paper. She giggles, then watches again quietly, then cries out with a laugh wanting to catch the lights with her hands as they move everywhere around the room.

Enrique turns over to watch me from the bed where he has just awakened.

"It's nice," he says, grinning at the scene before him. "You both look so lovely, so peaceful and I love the dancing light. What is that? A crystal or something?"

I nod. "Yes, it was a gift from a special old grandpapa I met in Cancun." "Well", he laughs, "it seems to be entertaining Theresa. She loves it. You would make a good madre, Charlie. Sí, I can imagine it. If only…"

"Shhh Enrique, don't say it." I move to the bed with the baby. "I don't want to think of it; even though I can imagine that life as a mother, you and I together. We can't speak of this because it can never be."

He drops his head in my lap, nodding in reluctant agreement. I hold the baby up so that she can walk tiptoe on the bed. Enrique teases and tickles her, Theresa now messes up his thick black hair. She starts to play with the pocket on his shirt, pulling it, hoping to find something to yank out. Enrique takes out a keychain from his pants pocket. Theresa squeals with laughter, as he shakes the keys; then shows her the plastic Mexican bull hanging from the bundle of keys; and then jingles the keys before her eyes. She is dazzled and giggles again. He hides the keys behind his back, convincing her they've disappeared.

Sneaky Uncle Enrique I presume," I say. I tickle him. Then he flashes the keys again. I can see that Theresa and Enrique have played this game many times before. Yes, I think, he would make an ideal dad. Life is good here in room 324.

As nighttime descends upon Havana, we remain in the hotel room, feed little Theresa some baby food and juice, and order some room service. I change her diaper, not that I even know what I'm doing; but I figure it out. Messy, but intuitive. Enrique plays with the baby as I pack my things and get the baby's change of clothes prepared for our journey tomorrow. I can imagine myself having a baby with Enrique. I dismiss the thought as quickly as it sneaks into my mind. Theresa falls asleep again around midnight and I place her in the baby rocker. A good baby.

The room is dark now as Enrique holds me close to him. I can hear the rhythmic Cuban music drifting up from the hotel café and the patter of the rain now coming down hard again in Old Havana. Enrique whispers, so as not to wake the little sleeping princess. "Charlie, it's not too late. You can still turn back. We'll think of another way to do this. I don't know, but…"

"Stop it, stop it Enrique". Although firm with my message, I say it gently. "Please, I'm committed to seeing this through just as I said yesterday. I am clear!"

He sighs, holding me closer, "I cannot argue with you Charlie. I want to see my sister happy but now I've developed such deep feelings for you."

"Yes, I have the same emotions. You know that." I change the subject. "Listen, listen to the rain. It's so gentle and hard at the same time. A place of contrasts 24 hours a day in Havana. I wish I had more time here for many reasons; but it's not to be." He cuts through me, touching my body with his skillful hands. I cannot speak, only feel him taking me to the edge. It's quiet now.

"Charlie, I will be on the plane to Miami with you."

I freeze, totally confused. "What, what do you mean?"

He sits up in the dark. I gush with joy, trying to keep to a whisper. "I'm so excited. That's wonderful. I'll feel so much more relaxed with you there."

"But let me explain", he says. "Just to repeat to you, we cannot communicate with each other, once we leave this room. We exit this hotel separately. Nobody can see that we know each other, in the airport or on the plane or in Miami. Any connection could get you in great trouble." Just a moment ago, I was elated. Now I'm deflated but I understand,

"Yes, y-yes, of course. Got it." Please, I think to myself, just hold me tighter. I don't want us to end, not now. But I can't say this to him. It will lead us in the opposite direction, cause me to consider wavering from my decision. I want to stay committed.

He nuzzles my neck and says, "Think of me as your guardian angel. I will be close by at the airport and during the flight."

I rest my head on his smooth, strong chest. "I don't want you to get caught Charlie, and I don't want to place Theresa in even greater jeopardy. I couldn't forgive myself if anything happened to either of you." As he strokes my hair, I feel him break down. He muffles his face in my hair to wipe away his tears.

"I love you Charlie, but remember that any link between us increases your risk, even upon your return to California."

"Yes," I say, "my life will click back to normal once I return home." I pause. "If we are successful, if we are successful," I whisper.

I awake to brilliant beams of sunlight shining across the room from the balcony window. The hotel room door bursts open. Oh my god, I think, what's happening? Geez. It's Enrique, and he's carrying a tray full of breakfast goodies and a newspaper in hand. Theresa stirs in her baby rocker.

"Hola, hola Charlotte Sweeney. A beautiful morning. I think it's a good omen." He places the tray on the bed.

"My hero. I'm ravenous. Thank you kind sir." I coo like a damsel in distress sitting on my knees on the bed; placing my hands on my heart in exaggerated appreciation. I think he likes my reaction.

"And now for a delicious start to your big day Charlie. Here we have the typical Cuban breakfast - Eggs, beans, bread, and plantains. Have you tried our plantains? We call them plátanos."

"Yum. They look scrumptious." Enrique picks one up and gives a little taste to Theresa, who reflexively spits it back out into his hand. The adults break up laughing; then the baby joins us in our hilarity as she watches Enrique stick a plantain into my mouth. "Plantains," he says, "banana chips, fried to perfection and then dipped in sour cream. You like?" Theresa giggles and screams with delight.

"I have died and gone to heaven," I reply. So good!" But, it's our last breakfast together."

"Sí. By the way, you look radiant in the morning. How do you do that?" He changes the subject. I feel anything but radiant, I think. My mouth full, I say, "Well, I eat my plantains everyday – very good for the skin."

He rolls his eyes. I gulp down another couple of fried slices of heaven soaked in the cold sour cream.

Enrique picks up little Theresa, throwing her playfully into the air. "My little niece, I will miss you niña!" He rubs his face in Theresa's chubby tummy as she wriggles with pleasure, letting out several more giggles. He gives her a small piece of bread which she thoroughly enjoys and swallows immediately, ready for more. It's only 8 a.m. We are having a great time.

"I guess I better get in the shower." I start to get out of bed.

The phone stops me. I freeze. It rings loudly, breaking our joyful mood. We both go quiet and stare at the ringing apparatus. I answer, "Yes?"

It's Miguel's voice. "Hola, Charlie. Please give me Enrique, I must talk to him immediately," he says with urgency. He sounds panicked, I think; handing the phone to Enrique. What could be going on now? We're just about to get ready to depart. My stomach is churning, sorry that I consumed too many plátanos.

"Miguel, qué pasa?" Enrique listens; taking in some serious news from Miguel. I see the tension take over his face. He grabs the newspaper which he brought in with the breakfast tray. It seems that Miguel is instructing him to read some article.

Enrique begins reading it aloud – slowly translating the words into English for my benefit. "Miami Customs Busts Child Smuggler." My head swims.

"What?" I put the baby down and give Enrique my total attention.

"Miguel, let me read it - the whole thing. Sí amigo, so Charlie can hear it first hand." He reads. "December 15, 1993. A man, David Ramos, was arrested at Miami Customs when he attempted to smuggle a three year old boy into the U.S."

"Shit," I cry out. My world is once again turned upside down, inside out with this news. Enrique reads more without any drama or emotion as his hope for Theresa's reunion with Marguerita dissolves into a fleeting dream. "Miami Customs found multiple problems with Ramos' forged passport. The boy's passport had a partial name misprint which immediately alerted the government agent." Enrique reads a little more to himself; then ends the article aloud, "Authorities are currently deciding whether to send Ramos back to Havana for trial. Fidel Castro has officially requested this. If returned to Cuba, it is likely Ramos will be subject to a lengthy prison sentence or something more extreme. Further sanctions to be announced shortly will be enacted by both U.S. and Cuban governments."

Enrique looks up from the newspaper, numbed by this update. His words are hollow. He looks exhausted. "You can't go." I pace the room like an outlaw grasping for an alternative plot so that I can still commit to carrying out the planned crime; even with the huge obstacles placed before me.

I can hear Miguel yelling, "Tell her, tell her Enrique." Enrique stares into my eyes.

"Charlie, we must abort. It is ten times more risky than yesterday."

"No", I shout. "I will do it anyway! My decision now." I am upset but re-adjust my tone as I notice Theresa starting to whimper.

Picking her up, I go to the rocker to soothe her. Enrique holds the phone, Miguel still talking non-stop. I have tuned them out.

Enrique hangs up and sits down on his knees in front of me. "Charlie,"he says gently, "we must cancel the plan. It was insane anyway. You were right in the first place."

Theresa's eyes have closed from the rocking. I put her down in her baby rocker; then go out to the balcony to get whatever air I can grab. God, it's so hot and humid today. The rain has turned into a light mist, creating an almost smoky, sultry ambiance. Enrique comes to me.

"Charlie, I'll call Miguel right back to confirm our agreement to cancel the plan." He holds me as I gaze out on a street scene below which has just captured my interest; my photographer's eye on auto pilot.

"Enrique, wait! Look down there on the street. I want to show you something".

"No, I must call Miguel first." He starts to walk inside.

"Enrique, just one minute, please." I touch his arm affectionately. He places his hand on mine as I hold onto the iron railing and point. "Look at that young mother, right there on the corner with her child. You see her in the blue dress?"

"Sí, I see her." I slide under his arm as we look upon the scene together.

"Her baby fell down and bumped her head. She was crying just a moment ago. Her mama quickly scooped up the little toddler and now she comforts her with her heartfelt mother's touch. Look, she's giving the baby a cracker or something, and smothering her with little kisses." I can see he doesn't yet see the connection with our current looming dilemma.

"Si, she is again a happy niña," he says matter of factly.

"Yes, a content child," I say. "Her mother has embraced her, giving her love and affection. She knows what to do to connect with her child, make her feel better, like nothing bad ever happened. We need to give your sister this same experience again, to feel that satisfaction received when you care for your own baby."

"No Charlie, this plan is cancelled. It's much too dangerous," he repeats.

I lose it right there, even with little Theresa dozing inside the room. I grab his arm and shake it. "Wait. I thought this was my decision to make. That's what you said. Are you bullying me? Am I still just a light switch for you to turn on and turn off?" He starts to speak Spanish to himself, really fast and furious; then stops and pulls me back inside to the bed.

"Miguel is an expert on this; even he is advising against it," he yells, locking eyes.

"Well, I am Charlotte Sweeney, big time, capable business consultant, woman of the world, and I say yes! Now, let's get ready for the airport!"

His anger erupts. "Loco, loco en la cabeza! It's not a silly game anymore. I lost Rita in a Cuban prison. I know this!, he shouts.

I look at him and now speak tenderly. "I know it's more dangerous than even yesterday, but I am willing to take the risk of prison or whatever comes. I think I can be successful, if I follow Miguel's wise instructions. Respect my decision. Trust me! Por favor?" I poke him now, playfully teasing. "I'm going through with it. No more arguments on this!"

Enrique finally nods, exasperated and holds me close to him. He can't fight me anymore. I extract myself from his presence and jump in the shower, ready to move forward despite the landmines ahead.

It's hard to say goodbye; but time is of the essence. I need to make this flight today. We just hold hands for a long moment. No words for our separation. No time for tears. I am amped up and ready to do this thing; the task now taking over both my mind and body.

"I'll secretly look for you at the airport," I whisper in his ear. He releases me and opens the hotel room door for us.

He kisses Theresa on her cheek and shakes her little hand. "Adíos little princess. Be good for Charlie. I love you both."

I head down to the lobby to check out – the baby in my arms, sending the luggage with the bellman downstairs ready to catch a taxi to the airport. After checkout, as I walk into the main lobby balancing Theresa in the awkward baby sling and rolling my suitcase. I've ditched my backpack and have a baby bag on my shoulder instead; stuffing my camera there with the diapers. I hear that familiar voice from behind me.

"Hola Charlie." It's Juan Jose and he looks totally perplexed. "Charlie, where are you going? Are you leaving?" I'm embarrassed to tell him yes. "But I thought you were here in Habana for over two weeks? Qué pasa Charlie and who is this baby? Where did you get her? Do you have a niña?"

Squandering for words, some explanation – I just stare down at him. "Uh – well it's a long story Juan." He stops inquiring; somehow knowing that this subject is off the plate for discussion. He looks hurt, like maybe he never really knew me like he thinks he did. "I'm sorry Juan; something urgent came up and I have to leave – go back to the states."

The little guy is down in the dumps now. What can I do? I manage to open my suitcase side pocket and produce a black and orange San Francisco Giants ball cap. Juan's eyes light up. "Charlie, for me? Gracias!"

"Yes Juan. I've been planning on giving this to you for the last couple of days. I just keep forgetting. Do you like it?"

"Like it? Charlie, Charlie, sí. It's my favorite U.S. baseball team. "Muchas gracias!" He's thrilled, putting the hat firmly on his head.

In my arms, Theresa beams down at Juan. She seems to like him and reaches to touch his head, acknowledging the cool hat. She's getting more and more comfortable with me as well.

"Juan, I must leave now to catch a flight. But I will remember you as my special Cuban friend. Don't forget me, okay?" Bending down, I give him a peck on his cheek. I want to ask him for his address, write to him; but I know better. If Enrique or Miguel knew I was even thinking of having Juan write down his home address, they would be in an uproar. Juan doesn't ask for my address either. He gives me a broad smile as I walk away, awkwardly managing everything in my arms and hands. I turn back to him to take a last look at this funny little Cuban fellow who despite his various family stresses, he has such an uplifting personality. He waves; then pretends to hit a home run for the imaginary crowd; tapping his hat in delight.

I see Enrique is already outside and has just hailed a taxi; with only his small carry on bag in tow. Handsome, he looks very tall, rugged and absolutely handsome. He was mine and soon will disappear from my life. I need to get used to that idea. How? The thought of never feeling his touch again, hearing his gentle yet masculine Cuban voice whispering in my ear, making my legs buckle beneath me. My adrenalin kicks in; and I counsel myself. Now is not the time for romantic remorse. Only one thing should be in focus! Theresa! He doesn't look at me even when his taxi begins to pull away; but I know he felt my presence, was really looking at me from the corner of his eye; and that he didn't leave before he was absolutely sure that I was following close behind.

Chapter Sixteen

STRANGER THAN FICTION

"**B**uenos días Señora," the Cubana Air check-in attendant greets me as I approach the counter. Theresa is getting heavier by the minute. I don't have a stroller with me. "May I have your tickets and may I see your passports? Your destination today is?" Okay, now's the time to keep it together.

"Miami – we're going to Miami, Florida."

"Sí, Miami, you are very fortunate. I hope to go there someday myself. I hear there's lots of clubs and dancing, and beautiful beaches."

I look at this young woman and notice that she is naturally beautiful. Long raven, blue-black wavy hair, large dark eyes, perfect full eyebrows, and very long eyelashes. Her eyes shine when she speaks her dream of Miami. Maybe she's a new at the airline and she's fantasizing how she too, can get on a plane and leave this country. She eyes the baby and winks at her, saying "hola, hola baby." She scans the passports with her eyes, ensuring they match the tickets.

"So your baby is Lisa? What a pretty girl. I love her golden curls." This girl is picturing herself a mother. Which one is more important to her? Having a family or going to Miami? I wonder for a moment. I wish she would hurry through this versus dragging out my very first step in this unnerving journey. Geez. I'm getting antsy; agitated. I try to make it obvious with my body language, that I'd like to get through this check-in process sooner rather than later. I notice myself gaining confidence as Nicole Ann Marie McCoy Sparrow. I could sit Theresa up on the counter; but then I'd be giving off reverse signals to this young woman; non-verbal cues that I'd like to hang out and chat. She notices the luggage tag on my suitcase. Oh shit! She puts her face up close to it to read it clearly. Confused and now speculating my identity, she questions me.

"Charlotte Sweeney? Why does your tag say Charlotte Sweeney? That is not the name appearing on your passport."

I hesitate, dumbfounded as to what to say in response. I'm freaking busted here. "Uh – well, that's my sister. Um – she lent me her suitcase. Mine was in bad shape. I- I guess I forgot to put on a new luggage tag with my name. Should I, uh, should I fill one out; this paper one here?"

"Sí, you need to have your luggage tag match your passport name. It is better. Can you please do this before I put your bag on the conveyer?"

I take the pen she offers me; my hands shaking like a windsock in a hurricane. I succumb, and boost Theresa up onto the counter, taking the weight off me, while I remind myself to fill the tag out using my new identity. Peripherally, I see that Enrique is walking away from his check-in counter. He's stalling, glancing at some magazine at the news stand not far away; probably wondering what the hell I've been doing all this time at this counter. I want to scream – "I can't do this!" and capture his attention. I resist the temptation. Finally, the young woman smiles and hands me the boarding passes and passports.

"Gate 22. Please go to the right and through Security. Thank you for flying Cubana Air." She waves goodbye to Theresa as I juggle my belongings and extricate myself from this first round of torture. Before I turn to go, I wait to ensure that she is releasing my suitcase; not holding it. Something in my head tells me that maybe she's secretly calling security or notifying airport officials; alerting them of her suspicion that I am not who I say I am.

I wonder if she's got a secret button attached to the wall beneath the counter that she can push at any time to instantly beckon the guards. Imagining two fat Cubans, armed with machine guns, one dragging me away and the other one hauling little Theresa off to some holding orphanage, I tremble inside. Instead, the young woman nods to the hefty male Cubana Air attendant - who grips my suitcase, lifts it and nonchalantly dumps it onto the moving conveyer.

As I walk away, Theresa squirms in the baby sling. Maybe she's getting sleepy. Time for some juice. God, let me first get through Security. I whisper to her. "Hang in there sweetie, I'm going to get you to your mommy. I hope." Enrique walks at a swift pace in front of me, pretending I don't exist. I yell at him inside my head. Damn it, turn around. I don't think I can do this! Maybe you were right. I have a bad feeling about the next couple of hours. But, I just keep on walking. If I keep moving, I won't crash with fear. The airport is jammed with people. A long line at Security. My head is full of conflicting thoughts. I'll make it. I won't make it. What about this baby? Blonde hair, blue eyes like me; but look at her skin. It's so dark; Cuban brown. Isn't it obvious she's not my flesh and blood? Crap! I'm supposed to remove my camera from the bag.

The security official checks the passports and tickets in my hand. He nods and waves me through. I put my purse in one plastic tray, the baby bag in another. I fail to remove the camera. I start to walk through the security archway. Shit! Someone taps me on the back. I jump. The uniformed security man pulls on the baby sling around my neck.

"Señora, that must go through the machine. Por favor, take it off." Fuck! I'm literally shaking. Are they trying to break me? Are they just putting me through all these motions, but know full well that I'm a total fraud? I gently pull the cranky, whimpering Theresa out of the baby sling and throw the contraption into another plastic tray. Agitated, Theresa now cries, as I hold her in my sweaty arms. My possessions glide through the short tunnel, no problem. The female security guard waves me to walk through the passageway. Thank you god, I mumble to myself, as I pass through to the other side and load myself once again with my heavy stuff. I trudge down to Gate 22 and fall into a black, ripped up departure lounge chair. Still fifty five minutes until take-off I realize as I examine my boarding passes. Boarding should be in about twenty minutes.

I see Enrique, sitting two rows away, reading a newspaper. He brushes his cheek while he stares at the print. I think he's signaling me hello, hang in there. I get out the juice bottle for the baby. Theresa stops crying; but jiggles around, wanting me to let her crawl and who knows, maybe take some first steps on the floor.

Oh, it feels good to sit down. Another tap on my shoulder from behind now startles me. It's an old man, with red checks holding up an American passport. What? Is it his?

"Sorry Miss – I didn't mean to give ya such a start but ya dropped yer passport by Security."

I take it and flip it open. Shit, it is mine. With one hand, I reach down into my purse to see if I have the two boarding passes and the baby's passport. Thank you God. I locate them. "Uh, thank you so much. I don't know how that happened. That would have been a big problem for me." He should only know how much of a problem I'd have if I didn't have a passport – this passport. The old man sits down next to me. Theresa fidgets and cries out to get down out of my arms.

"Hey there little princess, are yer getting a bit fussy with yer mom? Such a small thing to be making such a ta do." He tickles and teases her. She stops her yelling and squirming, completely thrilled with the attention from this jolly old man with his thick Irish accent. I'm still hoping he'd just go away. I just need to sit alone and think. How could I be so haphazard and drop my most important item – my counterfeit passport? I'm disgusted with myself; dreading further interaction with this stranger. I had been craving this small island of peace before my hair-raising flight. What if this man asks me a lot of questions that I can't answer?

The Irishman whips out his wallet and produces some small tattered photos of a lovely young freckled red-haired woman and two young boys. "This here's me daughter, Gillian, a teacher in Miami and thems her two boys, Scotty and Rory. Tough little tykes, balls of energy just like their grandpa. She lives in Miami fer three years now; with her American husband, Derek." I smile, feigning to be intently listening to every word. "You wouldn't believe it," he continues. "The lad is a professional football player. Well, if ya call that poofy game football; with all that gear and all." He chuckles; his eyes lighting up as he mocks the American sport.

Theresa presses down hard on my thighs with her little feet, gyrating her body, stretching her legs straight out. Geez, this baby is strong. I force a smile.

"I think she's now past her nap time and just over tired." I give her the juice bottle. She takes a sip and then tosses it on the floor. It rolls and hits the foot of an older Cuban woman seated across the aisle. She looks annoyed. The Irishman jumps up to retrieve the bottle, warmly apologizing to the woman. Theresa now screams into my ear. The old man hands me the bottle.

"Here ya go now, no harm done. Shall I go wash the top off for ya?"

"No, no, I guess she doesn't want it." I stuff the bottle into the bulging baby bag.

"By the way, I'm Mickey McCreary from Dublin, Ireland. Nice to meet ya." He playfully shakes the baby's little hand, trying to help me calm her down. "Well, if I can help ya in any way, just let me know." He laughs and tickles Theresa. It works. She starts her own round of giggles and follows every animated move produced by the Irishman's expressive face.

"Yes, she's a little darlin', that's fer sure."

Content , Theresa closes her eyes and drifts off to sleep. This jovial man means well. But honestly, I still wish he'd disappear and be replaced with someone who doesn't want to make friends and chooses to have nothing to do with me.

"So, we're all off to Miami then?"

"Yes," I answer with one quick syllable. So what's yer name Miss and yer baby's? Damn. I shouldn't be hesitating for a second. "It's – it's – um…Nicole Ann Marie McCoy Sparrow." I think he's puzzled by me stammering. Geez, why did I say the whole damn name? He chuckles and under his bright red shirt, I see his belly shake.

"Well now, that's quite a long name ya got there and this baby, I hope she got off more lightly."

I nod. "Yes, she's Lisa Marie." I glance up and see Enrique rise from his chair, chucking his newspaper into the trash bin; glancing my way as he walks around the perimeter of our departure lounge. He looks nervous; probably thinking who's that old man giving me so much attention?

"Such beautiful names for such lovely ladies," the Irishman breaks my attention on Enrique. "And pardon me fer asking, but what brought you two lovelies to Havana? Not a likely vacation spot for Americans, is it now?"

Oh god, I think, please how can I change the subject quickly? But instead, I just swallow hard and respond. "Well, my husband… he's a singer. Um. He's in a band, a rock band called *Sparrow*. You know, like my name." Damn. I didn't need to add, 'like my name' - did I? Trying to sound authentic, I hear the memorized data drilled in by Miguel spill out of my mouth. I must sound mechanical. I've got to loosen up.

"Lucas, my husband, has been touring in Cuba. So, we came along on the tour. We applied for special cultural arts visas ahead of time. All on the up and up." I smile, re-assuring him, and I raise my thumb to guarantee the validity of my false statement.

"Ah, and yer husband, where is he now? Must be a fool fer leaving you two beautiful girls on yer own."

Okay, I think, here I go with more regurgitated facts. "He's already in Miami. Uh, you see, my little girl Lisa came down with the flu - and that turned into a bad ear infection. Not good for her to fly per doctor's orders."

"Oh, well she's lookin' fine now, eh? But still a little cranky I guess. The little darlin'. You're a responsible mother fer sure."He pats me on my leg. Just about to add to my story, I see three Cuban policemen walk by, armed to the teeth with machine guns, hand-cuffs and batons attached to their belts. Geez, are those AK 47's? They stare at the crowd scanning across the lounge area, like they're looking for something.

I see Enrique stop in his tracks and lean against a pillar in the departure lounge, pretty close to us. He pretends to be reading a sign with interest but I can tell he's concerned with the police having appeared. "Are they on to us for some reason? My head is jammed with grizzly scenarios. Did that check-in attendant notify the airport police? I think the worst; wanting to bolt from this lounge and from the airport. I look at Enrique. He knows that I'm panicking. He brushes his cheek again as he stands there; then places his hand upon his heart; just for a brief moment.

A female flight attendant starts flirting with one of the good-looking, macho young policemen. She's petite and seems to charm him. They seem to know each other well. The two other policemen continue scanning the passengers, as if looking for something that requires their intervention; hoping to find any-thing. I notice other people starting to take notice of the armed police circling us. The flirtatious one joins the other two again, now looking as mean-spirited as they do.

An announcement grabs the attention of the crowd. First in Spanish, then repeated in English. "Flight 716 bound to Miami, Florida will board in about ten minutes at Gate 22. Parents with young children and first class passengers will be asked to line up in preparation for boarding. Please ensure that you take all of your belongings with you before passing through the gate." The three policeman are now lined up at a table right next to the flight attendant who will take our tickets. They put on thin plastic white gloves ready to do something. The Irishman said something. What was it? I was too focused on those policemen.

"Uh, sorry what did you say?"

"Oh, just wondering out of curiosity, how did ya get connected to a good doctor in Havana? Did they charge ya for it? Forgive me, I'm just interested in anything to do with medical care in foreign countries."

Oh shit, I think Mickey just noticed me looking over at Enrique. Does he suspect anything; and that's why he's quizzing me, asking me for details? "Uh, oh, the doctor, yeh. I got hooked up with a local pediatrician through The Hotel Inglaterra." Damnit, too much information for this Irishman. I didn't need to tell him what hotel I stayed in. I try to cover my discomfort with more crap. "It was very inexpensive and only steps away from the hotel. Quite convenient."

Processing my words, he looks satisfied. "Yes, I hear they got socialized medicine, like the U.K and like me own country - Ireland. A funny place – Cuba. Oppressive fer sure, but good healthcare. And I hear the education is mighty fine too; but people don't have the right food to eat. That Castro, I bet he's a bit of a nut and a bloody tyrant ta boot. Oh, please excuse my language. I just get carried away talking about politics and social affairs."

Another announcement from the loudspeaker. Boarding has begun. "Be prepared and understand that your carry on bags may be subject to a special table check by our local authorities. Please be ready to comply if asked to step over to the examination area." Damnit, I didn't expect this. Shit, do I have anything incriminating in the baby bag or in my purse? I have some credit cards and my driver's license as well as Gurjot's blue crystal stashed in my zippered jacket pocket. I just couldn't ditch these things. Enrique doesn't know that I didn't cut up those cards and get rid of them, which had been expressly demanded by Miguel.

"And will you look at that? Mickey complains. "It's the bloody Cuban police not trusting a soul. Can ya believe it? What are they hoping to find in them carry-ons? Stowaways?" Why did he say 'stowaways'? Was he referring to Theresa? I'm in my own private hell; in a frenzy of fear and paranoia.

I say goodbye to Mickey. He assures me that I'll probably see him again on the plane and adds, "I think from looking at your boarding pass when you had it out earlier, that I'm sitting in your same row – Row 15; maybe just across the aisle from you," he says. I feel uneasy about that statement from him; but graciously shake his hand before I hoist up all of my belongings. He helps me. Theresa is still innocently sound asleep in the baby sling; her body hot and damp next to mine.

I walk up to the flight attendant who is taking boarding passes. Will she just take my paperwork and let me get on the plane? Geez, I have a baby. I pray for it. No. She gestures for me to take my stuff over to the policemen. Oh my god. I'm freaking out. Was this all planned for my benefit; for the purpose of humiliating me and having me be an example for blatantly breaking Cuban law? Will I spend the night in prison; and who knows be reported dead by morning sunrise – just like Enrique's wife? Oh fuck. My heart pounds, aching to break out of my chest. The flirtatious policeman goes through my baby bag, removing every item. When he sees my camera equipment, he is very interested. Fuck, I didn't erase the photos taken in Havana. The policeman finally places everything back into the baby bag; then starts rummaging through my purse. Bloody hell, as Mickey would probably say now, if he were standing next to me. Is he going to ask me to take off my light jacket and un-zip the pockets? I hope not. He asks to see my passports and boarding passes. He still has my purse opened and my wallet is now laying on the table. He probably questions why there is no driver's license or credit cards in the wallet. He gestures for me to step to the side of the long table. What the hell?

Suddenly, one of the Cubana Air female flight attendants approaches us and signals that she will pat me down. It's the same woman he was flirting with earlier. Pat me down? While holding a sleeping baby? Geez. I put my stuff down on the floor, trying not to wake Theresa in the process. Successful, I then nod okay. The woman does her job superficially, without really probing or actually feeling for any objects that might be hidden on my body; just a light patting from my arms down to my legs. She just goes through the motions. The policeman waves his hand for me to go and return to the boarding area. He expression is stern - macho, still trying to impress the young woman. He reminds me of a rooster. They are one hell of a duo. Relieved, I race back to the line anxious to board. Theresa awakes, screeching in my ear, but grabbing onto me as if I were her real mom. We are still bonding; but she sees me already as her caretaker, her protector. I can feel it in my bones.

Oh God, Enrique is right behind me. For a second, I enjoy his proximity. I can feel his breath on me. I think he sighed emphatically to indicate that he is close by. The baby notices him and then I see that she's recognized him. Oh shit. Over my shoulder, she tries to grab his nose; just like they were playing with each other yesterday. It's their uncle-niece routine. Take the boarding passes, for Christ sake! I scream this inside my head. Finally, the woman takes them and rips them, removing only half the paper. I rush forward, trying to get Theresa away from Enrique as quickly as I can. On the plane, I find our seats and a kind man takes the baby bag from me, placing it in the overhead compartment. I put my purse down on the floor under the seat in front of me; still holding little Theresa, who is now awake and in a pleasant mood. I take a plastic green frog rattle toy from my purse and she purrs with delight. Then I get up, pull the baby bag from the overhead and get out some food for Theresa. I offer her a piece of cheese and wipe her juice bottle with a tissue before she gobbles up the cheese and gulps down every last drop. She is so sweet, jiggling the frog rattle with joy as her mouth sucks hard on the bottle. I already love this baby.

What a strange place I've journeyed to in my life. Here I am sitting on a plane originating from Havana, rum-running a little baby girl to a strange new place; and in love with a man I will never see again after this flight. I could never have predicted this strange array of circumstances. Theresa rattles her toy with exuberance; laughing when she recognizes the Irishman who tickles her as he greets her.

"Hello there little Lisa. Yer sure having fun already on this airplane." He sits down just across the aisle from me. "See, I knew we were sittin' pretty close together. Well, only a one hour flight to Miami. We'll be there in no time." I know, I think. In some ways, I wish it were a five hour flight so I have more time to practice my new persona before I go through U.S. Immigration and Customs. I continuously quiz myself in my head, just to make sure I've got down every detail; as I may need these at the crucial time. Enrique passes by our seats, without even a glance at us. He doesn't want Theresa to recognize him again. Good thinking. I know he's sitting just a few rows behind us. I wish I could touch him one more time. Feel his five o'clock shadow, which arrives around two o'clock in the afternoon. Have that chin brush my skin, irresistibly causing me to automatically tingle. I remember when we were together at Isla de Mujeres, laying together on the beach. He had tenderly brushed his face against my hand. It was about two o'clock in the afternoon. I had glanced at my watch as I looked down. His whiskered chin had felt soft and warm on my hand. Then, when he slid his face down my bare back, I wanted to cry out lustfully; but I controlled myself. Had he suspected what was going on in my mind? I close my eyes now, while I hold Theresa who continues to entertain herself with her plastic frog. That scene on the beach with Enrique feels like it happened months ago; not just 48 hours ago. Snap your fingers and your whole life changes, I think. I wish I could blink and I'm through U.S. Immigration.

My thoughts are interrupted by a huge German man, who must be 6'5" inches tall. As he looks down at mother and child, he seems very annoyed. "That's my seat." He points to the one next to me by the window.

He looks at the baby in dismay. I guess he doesn't like babies. Geez - chill out, I think. Lifting Theresa, I rise and come out into the aisle, letting him pass. He has a giant carry-on with him and tries to slide it under the seat in front of him; but it sticks out where his large feet tightly press forward into the black leather over-sized briefcase, as he sits down. I hope the flight attendant busts him. Why didn't he put it in the overhead? What a lug! When I take my seat again, Theresa starts to cry. She's frightened of him.

He starts talking fast in perfect German-accented English. "I hate this airline; inept Cuban stewardesses, bad service, unsafe pilots. I can't wait to get back to Germany," he complains. He stares at Theresa, who continues to cry. "Do you think you can hold your baby away from me, so she doesn't bother me? I'm going to read my book now," which he produces from his jacket pocket. "I don't want to be troubled while I'm reading Nietzche. Of course, it makes sense that I happen to be reading this German philosopher. Here's a fitting statement for today. He reads from his book. "What does not destroy me, makes me stronger." He quotes Nietzche, as he accusingly points to the now whimpering Theresa. "I hope this doesn't destroy me," he says smugly, thinking he's so smart and witty. He has no smile; only obvious annoyance.

Then he picks up his book once again, and ignores us completely. God, I hate pseudo-intellectuals; definitely, this is my number one hot button. Shaking the green frog at Theresa, I try to distract her from this nasty man. I am unsuccessful. Her whimpers get louder and constant. I quickly take out a second toy from my purse; this time, a plastic blue fish rattle. Go on, I think, shake it in that nasty man's face. She shakes it and I smile, even though she continues to fidget and cry.

Mickey sits across the aisle, looking concerned. I can feel that he wants to ask the grumpy German if he'd like to switch seats with him. Mickey reaches across the narrow aisle and is just about to speak to me when the flight attendant makes an announcement in Spanish; then follows in English, letting us all know that they will be closing the main cabin door; and we should all ensure that we are seated, with our seat belts fastened.

"Should I ask that man to switch with me?" he offers.

"No worries; like you said, this is a short flight. We will be fine." Geez, let's get it over with. I start to get a little nervous as we ready for take-off. My mind becomes focused on other, more dangerous thoughts. I squeeze the blue crystal which is still zipped in my jacket pocket. I can feel its distinct shape. For some reason, it calms me down as we lift off the ground. Thank you Gurjot.

Theresa falls asleep again as soon as we take off. It must be the motion and the ambient background noise. The German man looks happier. God, I wish I could go to the restroom. It's been five or six hours since peeing early this morning. Safely up in the air, the seatbelt sign turns off. I ask Mickey if he can possibly hold the sleeping baby while I run to the toilet. He graciously accepts and carefully takes little Theresa in his arms. She is heavy, especially when asleep. I thank him profusely. Enrique sees me as I walk to the back, passing by his seat. He feigns getting something from the seat pocket in front of him and touches my hand as I use the top of the seat for balance. Ahh that touch! It was just what I needed; to feel his skin one more time on mine.

In the toilet, I wash my face after I do my business. As I go to unlatch the door; I notice a small slip of paper sticking out of the bottom of the mirror. I look more closely at it. Oh my God. Written in light blue ink, it says: "I love The Brave One!" My eyes tear up. He wrote it. He wrote this special note that only I would understand. Am I The Brave One? Can I do this? Will I succeed or fall flat on my face ending up on the front page of The Miami Herald? I love that man. Do I have a pen in my purse? I want to write something on the reverse side and leave it in the same place. He could possibly return to the toilet and read it before landing. Damn it. No pen. I can't find one. Maybe it's better that I not leave a note in response; just in case someone sees both messages - and somehow puts the puzzles pieces together.

Passing by Enrique's seat, I dare not give anything away - but I can't resist. I make eye contact with him just for a moment and nod my head, hoping that he interprets this as me letting him know that I found his note. He flashes his award-winning crooked grin. I want to bend down and kiss him. I continue back to Mickey and the baby.

Theresa is awake and flirting with the jovial Irishman. "Can I just play with her a bit more? He asks. I don't have such young grandbabies any more and this little bundle is a real treat for me."

Still flustered by Enrique's touch, I nod, adding "Of course, Mickey." He nuzzles the baby.

"Oh, and here's your Immigration and U.S. Customs form. I got you the American rendition." He hands it to me, with a chuckle. "Uh – oh, thanks Mickey. Do you have a pen I can borrow?" "Yes, here ya go!" I sit in my seat and study the two passports in front of me.

I fill out the form stating that the only country visited was Cuba. In automatic mode, I write my name on the form. Oh shit. I wrote Charlotte in the section asking for 'first name.' Damn it. I panic; trying to flag down an attendant. It looks like no airline personnel are anywhere down the aisle. I need to get rid of this incorrect version immediately and get a new one. Pressing the red button by my seat to beckon the flight attendant, I wait as Theresa fidgets in my arms. It seems like it takes forever for anyone to arrive. The overweight attendant looks annoyed as she approaches.

"Is there a problem Miss?"

"Um – yes, so sorry, but I need another U.S. form. I misplaced the one I got earlier."

I manage an apologetic smile. "Right then, I'll be back in a moment with another one. We're getting ready to land and we're doing the final chores. So – please be patient, he says firmly."

As she leaves, I take the damaged form and rip it into tiny pieces, stuffing the fragments into a used yogurt cup from Theresa's airplane snack. Finally, the attendant walks by and then actually passes me by. No form. I turn my head to follow her as she passes to the back of the plane.

She suddenly turns, remembering that she forgot to give me the form; then hands it to me. "Here ya go, madam." Hmm, I think, she changed from addressing me as Miss to Madam. She must be annoyed. I carefully write my name and dependent's name on the form, stating that I didn't buy any souvenirs. Not supposed to spend American money, remember? I think this to myself. Don't screw up this second form.

Oh shit, we're landing. The announcement is made. "We will be touching down in about twenty minutes, a deep voice says loudly in both Spanish and English. That could end up to be my gate to heaven or to hell. Where's the dice? It'll be a crap shoot, I think to myself.

"Mickey, I better take the baby now. I need to check her diaper." He makes a face in jest.

"Oh. Right. Here ya go."

I take her into my arms. The German, overhearing our conversation, overtly winces - anticipating the worst; dreading the baby's return to his vicinity.

"Hello little baby. So nice to have you back here," he says sarcastically and makes a face like he just smelled something bad. He opens his Nietzche book and reads out loud once again. "One may sometimes tell a lie, but the grimace that accompanies it tells the truth. You understand?" He laughs like he's the lead comedian in the show and just performed his best joke of the night. "That Nietzche, he is a genius."

"Funny," I say without expression and offer a fake smile.

I can't deal with this blowhard right now. He'd turn me into the local police if he had a clue that I wasn't really the Theresa's mother, but instead an international criminal. Such pleasure he would reap being the one to turn me in at Immigration. We've started our descent and I rehearse the important identity details in my head. Nicole Ann Marie McCoy Sparrow, married to Lucas Sparrow, lead singer in the band called Sparrow. My daughter, Lisa Ann Marie Sparrow is eleven months old. We are without my husband because she caught an ear infection. She was born in

Ventura, California. I used to be a singer… Geez, just land the damn plane and let me make it or break it! We're on the ground. Don't freak out. Act natural, I plead with myself.

Whispering to Theresa, I say, "This is it baby cakes. Your time to be Lisa Marie." Oh shit! I think the German overheard me, wondering what the hell I meant. A familiar series of chimes ring out. Everyone rises in unison, and starts to pull out their carry-on bags from everywhere they were stuffed. The German starts to break out onto the aisle like a big bully. I let him go ahead of us.

"Bye Mickey, it was so nice to meet you." I smile in thanks as he hands me the baby bag from the overhead compartment.

"Well, I've had such a good time. You and little Lisa have been the ideal company for an old lonesome Irishman. Be safe me darlings, he says with his playful Irish accent. He plants a peck on my cheek and another on Theresa's head. She thinks he's starting to play a game with her, and bursts out with the giggles.

Leaving Mickey behind, I high tail it off the airplane, wanting to be the first to get my luggage and hit the Immigration area. The Agent motions me over to his desk. I'm shaking like a leaf; but happy to be ahead of the crowd. Theresa is holding onto me very tightly as I approach the agent with passports and form in hand. He's a crusty tough-looking man, with a gruff attitude.

"Names?"

"Yes, um, Nicole Ann Marie McCoy Sparrow."

"Yeh, and the child's name?"

"Um- Lisa Ann Marie Sparrow." Thank you God. I got it right.

"Why were you in Cuba? You know, it's not permitted for Americans without an advance cultural arts visa. I don't see one here." Doubting I have such a thing, he examines my passport again. "Please explain the reason for your trip."

He stares me down just like a tough interrogator would do when drilling someone suspected of committing some heinous crime. I explain the whole Sparrow band scenario and Lisa's sudden flu, which ended up in an ear infection. I should get an

Academy Award for this. I'm doing so well even under this man's severe scrutiny.

"I see," he questioningly sizes me up. "So where is your husband now?"

I try to quickly gather my thoughts. "He's- he's – um, in Miami waiting for us. He has a gig here tonight."

"A gig? You mean a performance?" He says this to emphasize the word 'performance'; letting me know that he's in control and his mission is to intimidate me.

"Yes, a performance. That's right. That's what I meant, sir."

He nods his head, considering the additional information. "Where is his performance tonight then?" He raises his eyebrows.

Fuck. Where? Geez. Miguel didn't tell me where the imaginary gig was to be in Miami. "Um – you know, I'm not sure. I think it might be a corporate performance for some big company." I'm grasping to think of something. "I – I think it might be at the Convention Center." I shut up and see what happens.

"Yeh, that's possible," he confirms that he believes I could be telling the truth. "Ven acá. Ven acá." It's Theresa. Oh my god. She's speaking Spanish. She never speaks full words; only gurgling and indecipherable pieces of words. Now Spanish? What the hell? Shit. I'm busted. I freeze, unable to speak.

Out of nowhere, a familiar voice yells out from right behind me. "There you are me darlings." It's the Irishman. "I've been lookin' everywhere for yers," he shouts out. "I thought I lost ya dear." He hugs me. He must have been standing right behind me and overheard Theresa's Spanish. "Oh my lord, the child is speakin' them Spanish words. Isn't she just amazin'? A little genius to learn so fast."

Mickey kisses Theresa and she laughs. "Ven acá. That's what she said," Mickey repeats the phrase like a proud grandfather. "I taught her them words meself." He takes Theresa in his arms as he smacks his passport down on the counter with his completed immigration form. "This here's me daughter and granddaughter. But I guess ya figured that out, right man?" Wow, Mickey is one bold guy.

The crusty agent looks perplexed. Theresa's outburst and Mickey's attempted rescue happens in an instant. I'm over-whelmed with anxiety and feeling nauseous. "You got grand-kids?" Mickey asks the agent.

"Yep," the agent says.

"You'd be proud too if yer grandchild memorized Spanish words in such a short time, wouldn't ya?" Mickey presses him, using his charm.

The agent nods in agreement. "Yeh, that would be some-thing. It is impressive for such a young child." He actually smiles back at the Irishman; then takes one more look at me. I wonder what will happen next? Is it going to be handcuffs or an inter-rogation room for me now; or has Mickey successfully beguiled this man?

The agent stamps our passports. Bang, bang, bang. He hands all of them back to Mickey. "Have a good day in Miami folks. Welcome back to America, land of the *free*," he emphasizes his last word and waves us on.

Walking through the security doors, I almost fall down, not quite having recovered from my distress. "God, Mickey, I-I-I just don't know what to say, how to thank you. How did you know what to do?"

He hands me the two passports. "Don't ya worry about it. Something was going on there, and I put two and two together. I don't need to know any more." Mickey smiles and hugs us both; then disappears out of my life as suddenly as he had entered it.

It's pouring down outside. I see the taxi stand area is almost flooded just outside the automatic doors. Rain seems to be a theme for me in the last few days. The baggage claim area fea-tures wall to wall people. Holding Theresa, and with the baby bag on the floor, I grab my suitcase from the carousel. I go through the customs line fairly quickly where they ask me if I've purchased anything – like Cuban cigars? "Nothing," I say with confidence. The man nods and waves me on.

Where is he? He's gone now. No more Enrique. Anyway, he only had a carry-on bag; no checked-in luggage. Relieved from the experience at Immigration and Customs, I now mourn the loss of my "should have been" life partner. My primary focus now is on little Theresa, getting her to her mommy at the hospital; and then handing her off to Diana Muñoz.

In the taxi, Theresa plays with the charm on my necklace, a sapphire set in a small 18 carat gold circle; a classic piece given to me as a birthday gift by Doug. The baby turns it over and over in her tiny hand, pulling it, trying to put it in her mouth. She's having fun feeling it's shape; it's smooth surface. I trace it constantly with my fingers when I'm thinking or considering the right path to an important decision. Theresa clings to me as if I am her mother. I don't want to leave her. My heart aches. Her crystal blue eyes are lit up today. Gurjot's crystal will always remind me of her exquisite eyes. There is a kind of serenity generated for me when I gaze into those sweet, innocent eyes. Theresa has become my savior versus the other way around. She doesn't suspect what's coming her way. Will she recognize Marguerita, her birth mother? Will she feel as comfortable with her mommy as she is right now, here in my arms? Will she ever discover the true story and hear about today's close call with U.S. Immigration? Will her Uncle Enrique share our short-lived love story with her when she reaches her early teen years?

Miami General Hospital is in view. We pull up to the entrance and I realize that I have no idea what to do with my big suitcase while I try to locate the cafeteria to meet Diana Muñoz. It's still raining; a light humid shower now. The friendly taxi driver carries my suitcase into the hospital lobby for me. Satisfied with a nice tip, he hands me his business card.

"If you need a ride somewhere later today, give this number a call. I'll personally take you anywhere no matter how hard it rains." He winks at me. "You got all your stuff, Miss?"

I nod and quickly turn to figure out the layout of the hospital complex. Is there a map someplace in this lobby? A receptionist chatters on the phone. It sounds like a personal call.

"Yeh, yeh, I don't like her either but I gotta go over to her house 'cuz she's my best friend's sista!" She says all of this with a heavy east coast accent.

Maybe she's a New York City or New Jersey transplant, I think.

"Yeh, I'm bringing some Danish. It's a brunch thing, so I thought that works, right?" I notice her nameplate on the counter, Roberta Myer. She's chewing gum and stops talking to form a big bubble, her popping noise echoing in the large hospital lobby. "Yeh, I think maybe they'll have some mimosas there. She's so la di da. I know! I know! That's why I can't take her! A wench! I know! " She breaks out into high-pitched laughter.

I take the opportunity to break in. "Sorry for the interruption."

So lost in her conversation, Roberta had no idea I was standing there and seems flustered when she hears me speak; like she's been caught by her manager goofing off on the job. "Gotta call you back Sarah." She quickly hangs up; spitting the gum into her hand and sticking the pink substance on a newspaper close by the phone. Then she transforms into a whole new character; which includes more formal diction and a definitive change in physical posture.

"Yes ma'am, can I help you find something?" I do a double-take. She must be a part-time actress.

"Uh yes, two things, please. First, where can I find the cafeteria? And second, is there somewhere I can leave this big suitcase while I'm here visiting the hospital?" She looks at the baby; sympathizing with my load.

"The cafeteria is on the 3rd floor and it will be directly in front of you as you exit the elevator. But, I regret to tell you, we have no accommodation for visitors' suitcases. I'm so sorry," she says politely. "I'm afraid you'll need to take it with you."

I guess I can do that. It's just so cumbersome, I complain to myself. She can see my disappointment. Exhaustion has overtaken me. I'm sagging. I start to walk away, heading to the elevators.

"Miss, Miss," she calls to me. "Wait a minute. Come back. You can put your big suitcase behind my reception desk. I'll watch it for you." I hesitate just a second, not completely trusting her motive; but I am so thankful for her offer. I don't want to lug that thing around in the midst of this important transition.

Before taking the elevator, I stop at the restroom. Time to change this baby's diaper. I hate to hand her off with a loaded diaper. That imprint will be forever in Marguerita's mind – the heroine who did everything right except hand over a smelly, dirty baby. I was right. That diaper needed changing badly. Brushing my hair, looking at my bloodshot eyes in the restroom mirror, having slept very little last night in Enrique's arms; I straighten myself out – ready to do this last step. I sit Theresa up on the changing table and sprinkle her with adoring kisses. "I love you sweetheart. Remember me, okay? Your fairy godmother." She giggles at me and nods her head. "Ven aca. Ven aca," I tease her.

She giggles and repeats, "Ven aca." I know I'm stalling, trying to enjoy these final moments with this baby, who now feels like my own.

A tall dark-haired, small-waisted nurse sits at a table in the corner of the cafeteria. She wears a nameplate telling me that she is, indeed, Diana Munoz. And there's the red rose pinned to her white uniform's lapel. The final stage of our plan is coming to fruition. She's reading a book and having some kind of hot drink. She looks at me as I approach. Jumping up like I'm her close friend or relative, she hugs me with gusto.

"How are you? And you - little baby. Ready to come to your auntie?" I can see that she's rushing me to do the hand-off and get the hell out of here; but she smiles and makes a big family reunion fuss the whole time.

I'm somewhat baffled, disoriented but I make sure that I give Theresa a quick and final hug. The baby reaches out for me, wanting me to hold her again. For a moment, it reminds me of leaving Priscilla's three desperate children; but then I suspect that Theresa will be in her loving mother's arms in a very short time. I start to leave and catch a glimpse of a stunning Hispanic woman rolling her wheelchair across the large cafeteria floor, heading directly towards Diana and the baby. Her eyes are beaming with joy as she races to get to them quickly. As the elevator bell pings and the door opens, I see the handicapped woman take Theresa in her arms, hugging her, kissing her all over. No cries from the baby. Diana and Marguerita look my way as I enter the elevator. I make a split second of eye contact with Marguerita as the elevator door closes. The image of the reunion and Marguerita's eyes overflowing with appreciation are forever etched in my memory. I have done a brave thing! I *am* the Brave One! Gurjot would be proud.

Chapter Seventeen

CRAFTING A NEW LIFE

T he year is 1994. The past twelve months have been a time
for re-inventing Charlotte Sweeney; revising my whole
existence. I returned to California from Miami; and cancelled my flight to Maui. Doug listened when I made the dreaded
phone call to let him know that I've had an opportunity to re-
think my life; what I really want to do with it. And it's not consulting. Without saying my heart has been captured by another
man whom I will never see again; instead - I just explained that
I needed some time to examine what I wanted out of a relationship. I couldn't lie to Doug. I confessed that I had experienced a
significant emotional event while I was traveling - so strong that
it caused me to re-think 'us,' and the idea of living together. "
For some odd reason, he didn't sound surprised nor did he seem
extremely let down. He just kept repeating that he wanted me to
be happy whatever it took; and understood my change of heart.
As I spoke to him that night on the phone, now several months
ago; I considered that perhaps he had decided to reconcile with
his ex-wife. I never asked him about this because it had nothing
to do with my decision to release Doug from my life. Sometimes,
you just have to go with your heart. And - my heart just wasn't
with Doug. We know where it lies; far, far away.

Many of those photographs I shot in Cancun and in Havana
are now framed and hanging in my new portrait photography

studio. You can look up at the walls as you enter *Clyde and Charlie's Studio: Photography At Its Best!* and see portraits of Lo Lo Lorena, Miguel, Juan Jose, Gurjot, Sunita; and even a shot of Enrique. But not the shot where the two of us are together. I have no captions or clues revealing that any of these photos were shot in Havana; but lots of people figure it out or at least inquire. I just grin at them, without admitting anything specific.

Portrait photography will not make me a million dollars; but the business has taken off nicely over the past year. I have intentionally left my workaholic high tech Silicon Valley past behind. Now - I keep two days per week free so that I can do something even more worthy than my photography business. Now a child advocate for the courts in Santa Cruz County. I represent children in trouble; case by case - where a youngster may be trapped in a home with parents who are drug addicts, alcoholics, mentally incompetent or even convicted criminals. Doing this pro bono, I feel like I'm giving back to the world on a regular basis; helping children achieve safety. When I succeed, I feel triumphant. What is even more rewarding is when I am given the opportunity to introduce the child to eager foster parents. Sometimes the abused or neglected child is frightened or angry, or maybe just numb. I guide each youngster through the foster care process, explain what's happening – hopefully, help them see the potential of a bright future on their horizon.

Today is the second anniversary of Priscilla's suicide. I'm in court, as the child advocate for a six year old boy named Roberto Jordan. His mother was picked up for buying crack on a back street of Santa Cruz; while he was ordered to wait in the alleyway for her. He stood there for three hours in the rain, without a jacket, while his mother went down the street negotiating her crack price with a local pusher. Finally, coming to an agreement, she grabbed the drugs and then forgot to go back to retrieve Roberto. Instead, she went home and shot herself up with crack cocaine. High, and in a stupor for hours, she remembers Roberto and hops on a bus back to the location where he was deposited;

but he was nowhere to be found. While she was gone, an elderly woman noticed Roberto standing outside, under her window and asked him what he was doing. It was almost dark. When the woman heard his story, she yelled down to him that he should come up to her apartment and wait inside because it was cold and wet out there on the street. She could see him shivering in his short-sleeve stripe shirt. He ran up the stairs to her open door. She had him remove his soaked-through clothes and gave him a fluffy oversized robe. She noticed a red bruise on the side of his face as well as a few other older black and blue bruises on his arms and back. When she asked about the marks on his body, Roberto admitted his mother had hit him the day before because he didn't want to stay home alone while she went out for the night. Last week, the same thing had happened.

"I just don't like to be left by myself for a long time. There's nothing to do and the TV doesn't even work anymore," he admitted. The elderly woman swiftly called the police, after giving Roberto some hot chicken noodle soup which he devoured like he hadn't eaten for days.

Hannah Jordan was taken into custody upon her return to the spot where she had deposited her son, Roberto. This was the fifth time Hannah was busted in Santa Cruz, twice before for buying hard drugs, once for petty theft, and another time for potential child abuse when a teacher noticed a few bruises on the boy's body. Roberto was in trouble and I was here today to help him. Mr. and Mrs. Lazarius, stand-by foster parents, waited outside the courtroom, hoping somehow that this time I would be successful.

Hannah had prevailed the previous four times when she had appeared before different Judges. She dragged Roberto home with her each time, only for her to continue her child neglect; wrapped up in her daily life of hustle and addiction. Still in kindergarten at six years old, Roberto had missed too many days to move him on to the first grade. Skinny, slight and with an obvious dark bruise still on the back of his leg, I want to take him home myself. Roberto is escorted into the courtroom and seated next to me. The judge has not entered yet.

"Hello Roberto," I speak softly. " My name is Charlie Sweeney. I will help you today with the Judge. Will you just tell the nice Judge what happened to you last night?"

He hesitantly looks up at me; apprehensive. I can see he's overwhelmed with the immense courtroom and the Judge's platform. The bruise on his face that I read about in the case preparation document is now black and blue. I see him spot the Judge's gavel. His eyes grow bigger. This environment must be scarey for him.

"Okay, I-I can tell the judge about it," he eeks out the words.

"Would you like to stay with your mom or what about living with some nice foster parents for awhile? I hear that Mr. and Mrs. Lazarius are very nice people."

I sense his feelings of guilt and conflict, as he sits there next to me. He looks down at his hands which are quivering in his lap.

"Could I go back to school if I stay with those foster parents?"

I smile and nod; placing my hand gently on top of his hands. "I'm here to help you and do what's best so that you are safe and well taken care of, Roberto. Yes, you can go back to school everyday."

Hannah Jordan appears at the table across from us. She is seated with a young male attorney, who doesn't make any eye contact with me or Roberto. The well-dressed man just stares blindly straight ahead; emotionless. I see him remind his client to stay seated as she attempts to get up, heading towards Roberto. She obeys and sits back down gesturing over to Roberto to get his attention. The boy looks concerned and his breathing becomes heavy. He stares up at me with his questioning eyes.

The Judge walks in. I tap Roberto on the shoulder and say, "The Judge is starting now Roberto. She's really friendly and will listen closely to what happened with your mom last night. Let me know if you have any questions. Just tap my hand and we can whisper. Okay?"

He nods. "Can I hold your hand Charlie? he asks.

"Yes, of course. We can hold hands the whole time." I take his hand in mine. The ceremony takes place with us all standing as Judge Mathias enters, raps her gavel and sits down. She gives Roberto a warm, sincere smile. But I realize that this is the same judge who sent Roberto home to his mother on the last occasion – two weeks ago. My hopes are dashed from the start. I've got to be strong and clear; objectively influencing the Judge, so we do what's right for this boy in distress.

Judge Matthias introduces the case. "All right…I'm ready to hear this case on Roberto and Hannah Jordan. I see that this is Hannah's fifth time in the Santa Cruz County Courthouse. That's not good Hannah. The child has new bruises on his face and body. This is documented by a medical doctor as fresh bruises; since we saw you and your child only two weeks ago. Roberto, I am Judge Mathias. Would you please tell us what happened last night when you were by yourself in the rain?"

I signal to Roberto to stand up so he can better see the Judge as she asks him questions. "Yes. I-I was told to stand in the rain while my mom went off to do something. She said she would be back in a few minutes; but- but, she never came back."

Roberto looks over nervously at his mom.

"Continue Roberto, it's fine," I urge him.

"But that old woman over there saw me with no jacket, and had me come into her house when it was getting dark and raining hard."

The Judge nods and further inquires. "Roberto, that bruise on your face, how did you get that? We need to know."

Roberto is on the verge of tears. "I- I lied to the police." A tear drips down his cheek. I put my arm around his shoulder.

"Roberto, tell us everything? It's important." The Judge encourages.

He swallows hard and nods while more tears fall to his mouth. The Judge asks, "Roberto, can you tell us what you mean when you say you lied to the police?"

I get up and take Roberto closer to the Judge's platform.

"Before my mom left me in the rain, she had me go into the baseball card shop and steal some cards from the behind the counter, while she talked to the guy. I didn't tell this to the police. That shop, it's called Hit or Miss. I-I-I took the expensive cards on the bottom shelf, a bunch of 'em and ran out of the store, like she told me to do."

My mind races as I stand closer to Roberto, holding his sweaty hand. I had no idea, and there was nothing about this in the report.

"It's okay Roberto. Tell us what happened after you ran out of the store," the Judge gently directs him.

"Um, well - she told me to meet her around the corner and give her the baseball cards. I was cryin' and she smacked me in the face. She told me to just stay there – wait for her. Then she to the cards and ran off. She yelled back to me that she would come and get me in a few minutes."

Hannah angrily yells out. "He doesn't know what he's sayin' Judge. He's always makin' up stories. He's just lyin'." Hannah's attorney pulls on her arm - instructing her to sit down, firmly counseling her to be quiet. Hannah shrugs him off but obeys; sitting back in her chair. I'm standing kitty corner to the Judge and can see Hannah's furious expression as she stares at her son's back. I'm happy that Roberto can't see his mom's intimidating body language.

"Judge, as you know, I'm Charlotte Sweeney, the child advocate for Roberto. If I may speak?"

She agrees. "Go ahead Ms. Sweeney."

I take Roberto back to his chair to sit down. I give it my best shot. "Your honor – the boy is of course, not on trial here. It's Mrs. Jordan who has broken the law numerous times, abusing her son and committing other known crimes. Now we find out that she had her son steal for her. She smacked him and left him standing outside in the rain for hours by himself, in the dark. Roberto needs our protection. Although Mrs. Jordan has been in the court four times prior in the last few months, she has actually been questioned by police on nine separate occasions in the last year for reported child abuse."

The Judge shoots me a stern look. "Well, I have only seen Mrs. Jordan on one previous occasion. I can't speak for other Judges who have reviewed her abuses or crimes, even though it all happened in this courthouse."

I feel doomed. The Judge is upset and apparently feels that I'm berating her. Damn, I think to myself. "Judge, what I'm trying to say, perhaps not very well, is that too many Judges have treated each incident as if it were the first time that Mrs. Jordan has hurt her child. Hannah Jordan's drug habit is also well documented. We can look at the file. She's not fit to keep custody of her child in the short-term and probably not in the long-term." Judge Mathias doesn't look happy. "That's for me to decide, as the presiding Judge here today. You understand, right? Please be seated Ms. Sweeney."

I drag myself back to sit down next to Roberto, feeling like a failure. The Judge follows me with her stern gaze. "I've heard enough on this case," she surmises. "Ms. Sweeney, I must admit one thing. Your summary of Roberto's recent past with respect to his mother was well-stated. I've heard enough on this case. I'm ready to rule. She bangs the gavel twice. "Roberto will be placed in the custody of his new foster parents, Mr. and Mrs. Lazarius, who I understand, are outside waiting to hear today's decision. Roberto will reside with them for six months, and then the case will be reviewed again; and I will be the residing Judge to hear this case at the end of the six month period."

I feel like dancing. I squeeze Roberto's hand and smile over at him. For the first time since I met him today, he looks like a hopeful little boy, rather than a battered ghost of a child. I hug him.

"Court is adjourned until one p.m. when I will hear the next case." The Judge rises and leaves the courtroom.

I bend down to talk to Roberto. "You did so well."

"So, I don't have to go back to my Mom, right? She hurts me."
I embrace him.

"That's right. Let's go meet your foster parents." As I open
the heavy courtroom door, the couple look at me with questioning expressions. Mrs. Dietz from Protective Services stands
with them. I smile and nod to everyone, confirming our success.
"Roberto, I'd like you to meet Mr. and Mrs. Lazarius. They are
your new foster parents." Again, I shake Roberto's hand and then
squeeze him one more time. I walk away, thinking – 'life is good.'

At home with Clyde, I'm feeling elated; but on the other hand
a bit in despair. So many children with their horror stories. I've
seen at least a dozen of these cases over the past several months.
It depresses me. Today, I was a champion. I am a Child Advocate.
It's never a fairy tale ending nor an ending of any kind. And truth
be told, sometimes it's better for the child to stay with the flawed
parent. Not this time! I am thrilled with today's outcome but
realize that Roberto is only safe for the next six months. There
is no guarantee after that. But I will faithfully follow everything
connected to the Jordans. I will be in the courtroom as Roberto's
loyal advocate. Pris would be proud of me. I can hear her gentle
laugh inside my head.

My mind wanders to the phonecall I made a week ago to
Priscilla's husband, Jack. It was the one spot in my life where I
hadn't taken any action. I was biting my lip, nervous what I might
get from the other end. When Jack answered, he quickly recognized my voice. He seemed subdued; and actually just listened
to what I had to say. I let him know that I was sorry I hadn't kept
in touch with the kids. Now that I left my high tech career and
had time to breathe, I wanted to see if perhaps Sam and I could
plan a visit to Florida; take the kids to Disney World for a couple
of days. First, Jack made various grunts and groans like he was
ready to give me a strong "No." Then, he asked, "What for? I
hear you're not workin' in your crazy job, but what's changed?
Haven't heard from you for almost two years." He paused. "Yeh,
ever since it happened; we haven't heard from ya. Why now?"

How do I explain where I'm at in my life without going through the details, which I'm not willing to share with him? "I see your point Jack. Let's just say that I've come to realize how important it is to connect with family, especially my two nephews and a niece whom I've yet to really get to know. So – how about it Jack?" I could feel him struggle with a response.

"Yeh, maybe that would work. Kevin was wondering what ever happened to his Aunt Charlie who never came back again. Anyway, my mother's moved in. She's watchin' the kids every day, getting' them off to school; making lunches and dinners. The kids love her. I'm just focused on work, makin' money to keep us good." I was relieved to hear his words and something about the condition of the kids. Jack still had his sharp edges, but somehow he seemed to be taking more responsibility. I recalled meeting his mom at Pris' wedding. She had seemed friendly and person-able; took my hand while Pris stood at the alter with Jack.

I remember her bending over and whispering to me in her Alabama drawl, "Priscilla looks so fine, such a sweet child. I already love her like she's family. My Jack – he's one lucky boy." I remem-ber my surprise at her warmth and her kind words. Perhaps her thug-like sons emulated her ex-husband who I understood spent some years in prison.

On the phone a week ago, I asked Jack if coming to Florida in the April timeframe for Disney World would work. He replied, "Yeh, the second week is when the kids have Spring break. So it's fine. I'll tell 'em, okay? Give 'em something to look forward to in a couple of months."

Our conversation was brief; but once again I felt that I suc-cessfully faced my fear of Jack like an angry dog, just as Gurjot had encouraged me. It took a lot from me to pick up the phone and call the #1 person I had blamed for Pris' death.

This early evening in late January, I lounge on my sofa, thumbing through this month's Elle magazine. I'm tired from shooting a big wedding all afternoon. I hear the rain thumping hard on glass of the skylight. Clyde brings me his green squeaky toy; wagging his long tail. He wants me to play with him. I throw the fuzzy octopus across the room.

"Catch!" Clyde pounces on it, snagging it in his mouth, then rushing back to me with pride - ready for another round of fun.

My cell phone rings out with Beethoven's Fifth. "Hola, my friend. What's up?" It's Carla. "Saturday night. Sounds like you are ready to have a rip roaring time sitting at home by yourself Ms. Sweeney. Are you still working now or what?"

"Just taking it easy. Yes, I was going to do some photography work tonight. Did a big wedding today. Challenging – cloudy and windy all day. " I can hear Sadie on the other end, barking at something on Carla's TV.

"*We* are going out tonight. A sexy new South American restaurant has opened in downtown Santa Cruz. Pinar del Rió. Have you heard about it? Latin music, scrumptious food. Carla smacks her lips into the phone. "Sounds yummy to me. Great write-up in The Good Times rag. Look, you haven't been out on a weekend night for how long now – months?"

I sigh, but admit, "I know. But I've got lots of things to do. Developing those pix and reading the next child advocate case. I've got another hearing on Tuesday."

She moans. "Oh-h - come on lady, take a break."

I open the sliding door on the balcony. The creek alongside my house is roaring, the water rushing to spill out into the ocean. "Listen to this, Carla." I put the phone out on the balcony. "There's a storm of sorts outside. Do you hear this creek? Might be the night it overflows. I shouldn't go anywhere. What about Clyde?" I hear myself with excuses and roll my eyes.

She's right, I need to get out. It's only a ten minute drive downtown. "Fine. You convinced me. So – the name of the restaurant is Pinar del Rió? What time shall I meet you?"

I love my work, but I could do with a social outing. And I haven't seen you for a couple of weeks." I hear the applause from Carla's end. She's clapping and yelling. "Hooray. I will buy you dinner! How's that for friendship? See you there at 7:30. It's just across the street from the movie theatre."

I appreciate that woman; trying to get me out of my curmudgeon habit of curling up on the sofa by myself night after night. We hang up.

Carla – she's still my friend. I've forgiven her for the Cuba misadventure; and admit that the experience changed my life forever. It proved to be a significant emotional event that catapulted me into a new way of life. From that point on, I've made all the right decisions about my life. And I've almost forgiven myself for Priscilla's demise; realizing that I was not in control and *could not* have been in control - no matter what actions I would have taken. When I first returned from Cuba, I stayed clear of Carla for a couple of weeks, until I ran into her accidentally at the beach. Just like old times, we both had our dogs in tow. Sadie, her dog, pulled Carla over to the frolicking Clyde. We stood there staring at each other, without words. I missed her, and longed to share my experience with my best friend.

Carla broke down in tears, right there, at the Rio Del Mar beach entrance. She couldn't speak, probably for the first time in her life. The self-assured, iron-clad Carla, stood there at a total loss for words. She seemed totally vulnerable. I grabbed her and hugged her, not releasing her for several moments. When I finally let her go, I could see her eyes overflow with emotion.

She asked, "You need to know that I was your friend long before my cousin asked if I could find the right person in America to help his family. I'm not proud that I didn't respect you more; confide in you from the start. Will you every forgive me?"

"Hmm, hmm. Maybe. You never know. The day may come." I kidded her; tried to lighten things up, while I was choked up with my own tears. She laughed; couldn't help herself. The tables seemed turned; me comforting her for a change. For the rest of the afternoon that day, I talked with her about Enrique, my experiences in Cancun and Havana, the wisdom of Gurjot, the sweet little Theresa, my journey to Miami and the Irishman who saved me. The dogs were in heaven, playing together on the sand while best friends re-connected. I don't think Carla's eyes ever went dry that afternoon. I was at peace with my own world and about to make all the important changes in my life. Already going through my metamorphosis; I was becoming a butterfly with a revised mindset of personal confidence and clarity. For the first time, I felt on equal terms with Carla; a good feeling.

Tonight, with torrential rain once again in my life, I venture out to meet Carla at the Pinar del Rió restaurant. No, I hadn't heard of this place before. But I'm hungry; haven't eaten all day. I can use some entertainment and intimate conversation with Carla. I take Clyde along with me. He loves the car. Parked in the overhead parking lot I pull out my umbrella, give Clyde a big chewy bone and walk towards the restaurant location. Crap, the wind is up, resulting in my umbrella turning inside out about half a block from the restaurant. Finally, the restaurant's neon sign appears through the pelting rain. Rushing inside, I'm a bit embarrassed about my coat – now completely soaked and holding my totally destroyed umbrella as water drips all over the polished wooden floor.

The hostess quickly rescues me, taking the umbrella and my coat. "I'll hang this for you. Oops – sorry about your umbrella," she sympathizes.

"Thanks. I feel like a drowned rat. I'm Charlie and I'm supposed to be meeting my friend Carla. I'm sure she has a reservation." The tall hostess reviews the list in front of her. "Yes, right. Your friend just called and said she'd be about ten minutes late."

"Great, thanks. Not surprised that she's been delayed with this weather. Geez."

She nods. "Nasty out there; but let me tell you – the food here is absolutely worth it. And your table is ready. Let me seat you. Just relax and get ready for a latin feast." I follow the graceful hostess. "Oh, and your friend has a special surprise waiting for you."

I spot a table in the corner, with two drinks sitting on the pastel printed tablecloth. Mint leaves are floating in the two tall glasses, which are full of a greeny-white liquid loaded with ice cubes. I sit down and the hostess hands me a menu. For the first time, I notice the background music. It's the Buena Vista Social Club singing softly, 'Dos Gardenias Para Tí.' I love this CD; and play it almost daily in my car. I'm addicted to the songs and beat of this music. Somebody comes up behind me.

I hear his voice whispering into my ear. "Buenos noches Charlie. I see you are drinking my delicious national Cuban drink – the mojito." Startled, I stand up and whirl around. It's him! "I came back for my English lesson. Can you help me with some American idioms? I think I might need several years under your care if I really want to…how you say…scrub up my English language skills?"

I touch his face in disbelief and look into his large twinkling dark eyes. "Enrique - that's 'polish up', *not* 'scrub up' your English skills." He shakes his head; then pulls me to him, enveloping me in his arms. He's still damp from the rain too! I'm quivering; reeling from this surprise. "Life is good Enrique, sí?" He gently helps me back in my chair, and sits down across from me, picking up the other mojito; preparing for a toast.

"Are you ready for life with a crazy Cuban hombre?" I still love this man's voice. "I don't understand Enrique, but what about…" He interrupts me. "Shh. My sister and family are doing well – thanks to you! He hands me a small elegantly framed photograph of Marguerita, Ferdinand and little Theresa, who seems to have grown from a baby into a radiant little girl. She has her uncle's crooked grin.

"And Marguerita is in remission; happy, raising Theresa. I couldn't stay away any longer Charlie. I've figured out a way to remain here, if you will have me. I'm willing to take any risk if necessary. We can figure it out together."

I'm emotional. I can't speak. I just nod and then I notice someone in my peripheral vision, sitting over at the bar. It's Carla, sporting her sassy smile - satisfied with her accomplishment. Whatever magic she has performed tonight, I'm delighted. She raises her mojito glass and gestures a toast to all of us.

EPILOGUE

FAST FORWARD 20 YEARS

The planned visit to Florida never happened. Jack phoned me back two weeks later, and changed his mind about my brother and I visiting the three kids. Sam thought the worst when he heard this, still believing that Jack was the cause of Priscilla's suicide one way or the other.

"See, that seals the deal," my brother voiced his anger and distrust. Nefarious Jack is hiding something. You see that, right? He's obviously scared that one of his kids will leak details of what actually happened the day of Pris' suicide. My bet is that Jack challenged Pris to do it; probably dared her."

Who knows, I thought. Even if Sam were correct, it would be good for us to see Pris' kids; not to lose touch. "You may be right Sam, but I'm going to keep trying to persuade Jack, reason with him. It's worth it," I insisted.

I called Jack every week for the next couple of months, urging him to see the benefit for the boys and the baby to stay connected to their mother's only living relatives. He finally refused to even take my calls. Then, one night he left me a voicemail stating that it was just too depressing for the kids to see anyone connected to Pris; and especially us. His family needed some space to move on and start a new life. He ended his message with a cold request for me to not to call him again or contact him in any way. Damn him! What a selfish man! The reality was that I knew that I had to accept his decision and let it go; or torture myself with continuous calls despite him ignoring me. Be thankful that I'd started a new life in so many ways, helping children in my community and building a long-term relationship with the man who mattered the most to me – Enrique.

Now 20 years later, I receive a message via my Facebook account from a female named Tanya. I don't recognize the name at first. She requests us to be friends like so many people do with strangers on social media sites. Then the words come into focus in her personal message; hitting me like a freight train. "I think my mom was your sister Priscilla. I am her daughter and now 23 years old. "God damn – it's Pris' baby girl. She's searching for me. Shock strikes me with hurricane force. I'm nervous and excited all at the same time; ambivalent. I shift to feeling hopeful; my faith restored in our potential reunion. My heart pounds. I see Tanya's Facebook profile photo. She is beautiful. She has Pris' smile and her eyes, her lean body and her thick hair.

When I call my brother to let him know about Tanya, he cautions me. "Why now, Charlie? Leave it alone. It's too late. Why drudge up the painful past? Sam takes a breath and almost growls into the phone. "I don't advise it," he continues on the same channel.

Enrique comforts me that night and as usual encourages me to do what is in my heart. "First, visualize how magnificent it can be to see Priscilla's bambina and then think of the worst thing that can happen if you connect. Then, make your decision," he says in the dark, as we gaze at the stars and the full moon through the skylight above our bed. He continues, "What if our son did not know his real mother? Wouldn't you want him to know about you if you had died? Know what you were like, about your life?" My Cuban husband turned out to be so wise.

I open the drawer to the bedside table and take out the blue crystal gifted to me so many years ago from Gurjot. I hold up the object as high as possible as we lay there together. The light of the moon catches one facet of the crystal. It glistens and twinkles; and we both "ooh and ahh' in delight. Then, we erupt into giggles, both noticing our still active playfulness. Even in our 50's now, we're still kids.

"Charlie, I think you have your answer. Sí? He stares at the crystal. A message from beyond. What do you think?" Enrique shifts onto his side propping his head on his hand, staring down at me; still interested in every feeling and thought I have. "I think I love you Enrique. Sweet dreams baby."

The next morning, I crawl out of bed before Enrique wakes and rush to my computer to respond to Tanya's Facebook message. My heart is already opening up like a spring tulip ready to burst with color for my niece. She responds quickly. "It *is* you!" she writes.

"Can you tell me anything about my birth mother? Anything! I have no information. My dad never talked about her since her death; not to me and not to my brothers who were scared to mention her. It was like she never existed. My stepmother only says bad things about her. But your sister was my mom, my real mom; and I want to learn all I can about her. Can I call you on the phone Aunt Charlotte? Can I call you my Aunt? Sorry – if I'm jumping the gun."

"Yes, of course. Phone me any time. With love, Aunt Charlie," I write back. When I hear the phone ring, butterflies take flight in my stomach. Oh shit! I quiver with fear. Why am I feeling this way? We talk for over an hour. Tanya is animated and passionate. "I want to meet you. Please, can I visit you in California or maybe you can come up to Seattle?"

I listen; flattered that she very much wants to meet me. I still have my doubts. Is this the right thing? Is Sam right; maybe it's just too late, I think to myself. For some reason, I revisit the place in time 20 years ago when I felt lost, still grieving the tragic loss of my only sister. When I first hear Tanya's voice on the phone, the hurt creeps in from the past, breaking the surface all over again. That sensation lasts for less than a minute; and then my mood completely changes. I'm uplifted - learning about my niece as she chatters on at a fast clip. I can sense her nervousness. I find out that she enjoys cooking when she starts asking me if I like to cook. She talks about the pork loin she just made using two different kinds of grapes – red and green. Strange, since I just made pork loin for the first time a week ago but with apples, onions and Calvados - my favorite French liquor.

"Both foodies," she says. That's so great. I love it!"

Tanya has the gift of gab, telling me secrets about her new boyfriend of just six months. "I think maybe he's too handsome and he's a writer, teaches poetry at two community colleges. So smart and eight years older. Sometimes I wonder what he sees in me. I'm just an ordinary grad student and waitress. But I love what I do. Maybe I shouldn't take our relationship too seriously. What do you think Aunt Charlotte?"

I love her uninhibited demeanor. It instantly reminds me so much of Pris. She's already asking me advice on love. I encourage her to give the relationship with her boyfriend more time to percolate. Perhaps, things will become clear for her after a few more months. She's hungry for my thoughts; digesting every crumb – considering seriously everything I say; savoring our delicious new connection. Then I learn that Tanya loves music and dance just like my sister did; Pris – a jazz dance major before she got pregnant, quit school, and then married Jack. Tanya's warm personable nature sweeps over me like a "full of life" blanket of Pris. A enhanced sense of peace and happiness flows through my heart as Tanya passionately describes the various details of her young life.

After making arrangements to fly to Seattle, I almost change my mind twice before my departure date. I struggle with my fear of the unknown. What if Tanya is actually angry and she's been hiding it all these years; ready to unveil it once I land in Seattle – on her own turf. Or - what if she has her evil father waiting for me, whom she really adores; plotting to get me alone and unload his hateful feelings towards our family? Each time these thoughts slither through my mind like a poisonous snake, they also vanish within 24 hours – replaced with genuine excitement about meeting the youngest of Pris' offspring 'in the flesh.'

A petite, pretty young woman greets me at Seatac Airport. In person, she is even more a replica of Priscilla than I imagined; with her dark hair and large deep brown eyes. When Tanya slides into the driver's seat, I notice her hands and fingers – tiny, slender and graceful as she moves; just like Pris. I feel the spiritual presence of my sister in the car, escorting us to the brink of a weekend where we will share the painful past and create the foundation for our future.

Tanya introduces me to everyone in her life – her friends, her boyfriend, her co-workers. She is so proud of her accomplishment – finally finding an important link to her heritage – me! I feel like I have a family purpose, probably for the first time in my life. We walk the food markets and museums in Seattle, arm in arm; thoroughly enjoying ourselves. With so much in common; even down to both ordering mint chocolate chip ice cream and gourmet egg dishes – our favorite things to eat. At the art museum, we are both attracted to paintings by Mary Cassatt; the artist's children clad in pastel swimwear playing on the beach, their mother sitting close by the shore. We gaze at this work of art for several minutes – silence between us. Tanya reaches for my hand as we sit on the bench and admire the painting.

We laugh as we shop together at our number one favorite clothing store – Anthropologie; picking out clothes for each other; trying on several items. While Tanya changes in the dressing room, I buy her a cloth-covered blank recipe book, where you can insert your photos of your own food creations and record each special recipe.

Later, we cry during cocktails when I reminisce about special times with Priscilla, like when she hid my diary in the closet to tease me but later confessed that she didn't really read it. "At least can I read a little bit?" eight year old Pris pleaded with me. I caved in and let her read just one page. Then, as if I had shared the greatest story every told, Pris asked me all kinds of questions about my writing. Why this? Why that? I felt like a great author at the time; explaining the rationale behind my innermost, private thoughts to my little sister. Tanya's eyes widen with interest as I share childhood stories. She hangs on every morsel of information relating to her birth mother. Honestly, I didn't realize that I still even remembered those little scenarios of Pris.

Tanya and I seem to bond less as niece and aunt; but more like sisters, catching up after a long separation. An easy comfort level, a natural syncopation quickly develops between us. Our relationship is racing with the wind as we reveal more and more about ourselves. "She's lovely Pris," I think to myself, as we walk down the Seattle street. "You would be so proud of your daughter."

THE END

ABOUT THE AUTHOR

Linda S. Gunther lives in Aptos, California, with her husband and her rambunctious springer spaniel. Growing up in New York City and then, after teaching school in the Bowery while attending Columbia University graduate school in Counseling Psychology, Linda escaped N.Y.C. for a different lifestyle on the West Coast. A year later, Linda was given the opportunity to spend a summer in London where she studied child development. After six weeks in Great Britain, Linda decided to take a giant leap and start a new life there where she later married an

Englishman, gave birth to her son, attended graduate school in psychotherapy and counseled parents and children in the west London suburb of Southhall; a community predominantly populated with immigrants from India. With a certificate in teaching English As A Second Language, Linda spent summers conducting classes for European business people who wanted to learn American English.

After six years in London, Linda returned to California and accidentally fell into a new career in Corporate Human Resources-landing her first job working for an international high tech company. Linda has held key leadership positions in some great Silicon Valley companies. This career provided Linda with the opportunity to travel the globe, delivering management development training programs and consulting with some of the world's brightest talent. Linda also became a part-time actress and has performed several roles in numerous Northern California theatre productions. She auditioned and was accepted to study with Yale School of Drama and the British American Drama Academy at Oxford University where she learned from great English actors including: Jeremy Irons, Vanessa Redgrave and Brian Cox.

In addition, Linda has been an avid explorer of cultures, embarking on a variety of educational adventure trips over the years, including: studying French language in Paris, portrait photography in the Soviet Union, Italian language and culture in Florence, writing for screen and television at UCLA, and a photographic journey to Havana, Cuba. Her passion for travel and continuous learning fuels Linda's fire for creating colorful fictional characters and story lines for both books and theatrical productions.